FALSE START
A ROB MARSHALL PREQUEL

ED JAMES

Copyright © 2022 Ed James

The right of Ed James to be identified as the author of this work has been asserted in accordance with the Copyright, Designs and Patents Act 1988. All rights reserved.

No part of this publication may be reproduced, stored in or transmitted into any retrieval system, in any form, or by any means (electronic, mechanical, photocopying, recording or otherwise) without the prior written permission of the publisher. Any person who does any unauthorised act in relation to this publication may be liable to criminal prosecution and civil claims for damages.

This is a work of fiction. Names, characters, businesses, places, events and incidents are either the products of the author's imagination or used in a fictitious manner. Any resemblance to actual persons, living or dead, or actual events is purely coincidental.

Cover design copyright © Ed James

CHAPTER ONE

The wind outside was howling like an army of wolves enacting some freaky mating ritual. Another rattle of the window, like someone was thrown against it.

Sammy Irvine got up and the room swam around him. He kicked away the pizza boxes and staggered over to the window. He swept the net curtain aside and looked out into the night.

He couldn't see anything out there beyond his lit-up veranda. Windy, but not as bad as the night he first got here, when some of the bigger trees tumbled over and just missed a couple of caravans further out than his. Two months on and they were still uprooted and lying there. That cheeky wee sod Gillespie hadn't cleared them. Lot of good timber gone overnight, he'd moaned. Still, Sammy wasn't complaining – one bright morning spent with his pocket chainsaw had got him enough logs to last him through next winter too. Not that he'd be here, but still.

The lights dyed the piled-up snow yellow like smoked haddock a couple of days past its sell-by date. The worst of it built up around the table and chairs, making it look like some snowmen were playing a serious game of Texas hold 'em. Hard to believe that a few weeks ago it would've been real people out there, with high stakes. Booze flowing, music playing, laughter. Now, the caravans opposite were empty, not that he could see into any of them. Couldn't quite figure out how it'd been managed, but he wasn't knocking the fact nobody could look in on him either.

Still, he wished for company. Longed for it. Another person to talk to, to listen to. To share war stories. Didn't have to be deep and meaningful, just... a bit of humanity.

At least the air would be fresh outside. Inside, it stank – the bin was full and the last two bags were piled up like the snow outside. He just couldn't get enough of those kids' crisps. Still on offer in Ashworth's, that prickly tang was too tempting.

He knew he should've taken the bags to the big bins when he went out earlier, but he'd got lazy. Complacent. Story of his life. At least he'd been out and stocked up – the cupboards were filled with tins of soup and enough long-life rye bread to see out the rest of the season.

Sammy took one last look out there. The only movement was the white-noise swooshing of the wind rattling the trees. He was the only one left here, the only one who still needed to hide in January.

The only one with nothing in his life.

Aye, keep focusing on the negatives, why don't you?

Sammy topped up his glass, all milky white from fingerprints. The gurgle of a free pour of vodka and the hiss of clear lemonade splashed in on top.

That big bluebottle buzzed around the kitchen. The *bane* of his life, that big bastard somehow avoiding the thwack of his rolled-up magazine. He took another shot at it and killed it.

Then the little shit buzzed off through to his bedroom.

The place still had that stale reek of gas. He'd checked the cooker and it definitely wasn't on, but the pong just hung there. He remembered one of the few chemistry classes he'd bothered to attend at school, where the teacher said they made the gas stink like that so you knew you had a leak. And it absolutely did.

Minging. But he couldn't detect anything. Not that he was an expert.

Sammy took the glass and sat down in his chair. Despite this caravan being an absolute midden, it had one thing going for it – a stove. Someone had taken the trouble to install one of those Norwegian jobs. Shove enough wood and coal in there, set it alight, and that was you for the night. Bliss. Made the whole caravan all roasty-toasty, so it did.

He stared at the telly.

The big guy caught the other one under the arm and threw him clean over the ropes, landing with a clatter on a table. He stood there, arms out wide, eyes closed, muscles glistening, bowing for the crowd.

They were booing him. Drinks cartons filled the ring, second-hand juice spraying all over him. He ran, bouncing off the opposite rope, then thundered across the ring and launched himself over the top, aiming for his opponent.

But he missed.

Didn't hit the deck straight away, either. He landed on a metal barrier, the steel crunching into his chest, and went down like a sack of coal.

Christ, was he *dead*?

Sammy didn't know, but it made him lean forward

on his armchair, elbows digging into his thighs. Too focused to even *think* about taking a sip of vodka.

The other one – the boy in pink and lime green, the one who'd been chucked over the top – managed to haul himself up to standing.ABizzy from destroying the table he'd landed on. But he was starting to come to. Managed to get the big one up to standing, then rolled him back into the ring.

Because he had to pin him *inside* the ring, didn't he?

Smart cookie!

Sammy reached over to grab his glass of voddie and took a deep drink of it, a few gulps. Burned at his throat a bit – just the bloody ticket!

He was still sniffing, though – that voddie wasn't clearing this cold like that Polish boy he used to knock around with said it would.

Still, Sammy didn't get much of a hangover from this stuff, surprising given the quantity he was putting away. He tipped the last of the bottle into his glass. Sod the lemonade.

A thump on the door.

Shite.

He tried to pause it, but it wasn't having it. The big guy was on his back, legs in the air, the other boy pinning him to the mat.

Sammy walked over to peer out of the window again. Dark, just thin light. Wind blowing the trees.

Nobody there.

He picked up the phone from the arm of the chair and put the SIM card back in. Waited for it to boot up.

No messages.

No missed calls.

Great.

Must've been a stray branch thrown through the air.

Another thump on the door.

Everything clenched in him.

Sammy was minding his own business here, and that included not answering the door after dark. It was just him, his vodka and several hours of WWE wrestling.

Aye, just ignore it.

Somehow the fight was still going on. He stood there watching it, holding his hands against the stove to warm them until they were nice and toasty. Keyed up, not just by the voddie. Kept glancing at the door and window for signs of movement. He picked up the glass and took another glug, almost retching at how strong it was.

Another knock. 'I know you're in there!'

In the name of the wee man...

Sammy put his glass down and wandered over to the door. Stuck his peeper up to the peep hole.

Man. Thirties. Long hair in curtains, deep scar on one cheek, cowboy jacket with all those daft tassels.

Nope.

Sammy sat back down again and took a sip of voddie. Glass was empty again. Didn't recognise the boy, so this was one to wait out. He picked up another bottle and unscrewed the lid, then—

Another thump. 'Sammy, come on! It's freezing out here!'

He knew his name...

Who the hell was he?

Another thud on the door. Then another.

Aye, and he knew Sammy was in.

All that smoke from the fire was giving him away!

Crap.

He got up and padded back over, then opened the door to the security chain. 'Can I help you, pal?'

The bloke was taller and fatter than he'd expected. Big guy, with a real presence. He was wagging his finger at Sammy like they were old pals. 'Thought I recognised you.'

Well, that was something he had on Sammy.

'Aye? Don't know you, pal.'

'Come on, Sammy. You do. Of course you do, you daft bugger!'

Despite the heat in the room, Sammy got a right shiver up his spine. Where did this guy know him from? Where *could* he know him from? Millions of possibilities and very few of them were positive.

'You've got me at a bit of a disadvantage here, mate.'

'Come on, man! You were shagging my wee sister. Kelly.'

Christ. Kelly...

Well, the apple had fallen a few fields away from the orchard.

'Oh, aye. Kelly. She was a smasher.' Sammy gave him a wide smile. 'Didn't knock her up, did I?' His laugh was too much, even he knew that. And he hadn't seen her for three years.

'Hardly!' The big bugger bellowed with laughter. 'Couldn't get it up, what she said. Mind if I...?' And he barged past, getting into the caravan. No stopping a boy that size, was there? 'Roasting in here! That fire's amazing and, ooooh, you've got one of them stick things, eh? All the channels for free. Mad into wrestling, me. Who's fighting?'

Sod this, no way was he letting this boy stay.

Sammy shut the door and walked back over. He

reached for the remote and turned off the telly. 'I'd offer you a wee drink, pal, but I'm expecting company.'

'Oh, I'll be fine. Won't notice I'm here.'

'*Female* company.'

'Aye? You cannae get hard, so that's not going to be a problem! And I could show you how it's done!'

Sammy was blushing. 'That isn't true!'

Of course it was true. And he knew. But how much did he know? Was he really Kelly Templeton's brother?

Sammy sat down. He needed more vodka, more lemonade but he didn't want to turn his back on him and go over to the fridge.

The other guy – Christ, what *was* his name? – snatched the remote and put the telly back on. The WWE was still playing. The big lump had turned the tables and was pounding the wee lad, trapping him against the turnbuckle.

'It's Paul, by the way.'

'What is?'

'My name. Paul Templeton.'

'Oh, right. Aye.'

'According to that chancer, Gillespie, it's just you and me here the now. In this whole caravan park. Two lads among hundreds of empties. Have to be mental to stay here at this time of year, in this temperature. Makes me think we're both in the same boat.'

Sammy picked up his empty glass. 'Aye, and what boat's that, then?'

'It's not a wee dinghy, I'll tell you that for nothing.' Another loud laugh, eyes locked on the telly. 'We're both hiding here.' He looked over at Sammy. 'Who are you hiding from?'

Was he really Kelly's brother?

Christ, was this guy a cop trying to sniff him out? Or was he someone Sammy had done wrong by? Could he be connected to the people he was hiding from?

Neither possibility was good.

'You first, big man.' Sammy took a slug of vodka. 'Who are you hiding from?'

'Cops. Post office robbery in Troon last month. Harder to come by these days, what with all that internet stuff and what have you meaning so many of the buggers are being shut down. Thing is, if you can find yourself a good one, it's well worth it. No guards and tons of cash. Price of stamps these days too, man – if you get a ton of them you can shift them like nobody's business.'

'Worth it even if you have to hide out down here?'

'Oh aye. Cleared a hundred grand in cash too. I'll hide out here until the spring and put some feelers out. Hopefully the heat will have died down by then. Head back to

Glasgow, sell the stamps and spend my money. Or if the heat's still on, might take myself away on a wee holiday somewhere warm. Get a ferry to Spain or Holland.' He snorted, then rubbed at his septum. Checked it was still there. 'Now I've told you my life story, why are you here?'

Sammy wanted another voddie, even though he was feeling pretty pished. And he had a stranger in his house. Not a good combo. 'Actually just fancied a wee break from all that.'

'All what?'

'Ach nothing. City life.' He raised his glass. 'If you're not buggering off, do you want a—'

'Sure it's nothing to do with killing him.'

Said it so quietly it was like he barely said it at all. One of those things where Sammy could've imagined he was saying it.

'What was that, Paul? Didn't quite catch it.'

'I said, you hiding here has nothing to do with you killing John?'

Shiiiiiite.

What had he been thinking letting him in?

Guy was a total stranger!

'John who?'

'The John you killed.' Paul picked up the empty vodka bottle and tossed it in the air. He caught the handle, brandishing it like a club, then swung at Sammy's head.

It battered off his skull and he fell back in the chair. Paul grabbed his hair and hauled him to the floor.

Too pissed to get up. Too drunk to fight him off.

'I haven't killed anyone!'

'You fucking did!' Paul was still holding the bottle. A thick red mark smeared the bottom. 'John was my cousin!'

'I don't know a John!'

'John McStay!'

Shiiiiite.

'Come on, mate, it wasn't—'

Clang.

Another thwack with the bottle.

Sammy went down face-first. A nail from the floorboard dug into his cheek, tearing at the skin under his eye. He felt a bump growing on his head already.

Everything swum around – and not in a good way.

Big Paul was looming over him. 'You're going to pay for what you did to him!'

'Listen, I don't know a John McStay!'

'Thing is, pal, I know your face from Inner Space.'

The nightclub Sammy ran through there.

Bit too much Charlie and not enough Sammy.

'Saw you chatting to Wee John in there, so don't

fucking lie to me!' Paul swung the bottle back, then lashed it forward again.

Sammy managed to duck out of the way.

The bottle crashed into the table and sent everything flying off. The remote hit the wall. The glass rolled onto the floor, smashing into a few pieces.

Glass went everywhere.

Sammy grabbed the heavy base in his right hand. The good one. Spiky shards pointed out.

Paul thundered towards him and kicked the glass. Staved Sammy's hand. Followed it up with a right hook, sending Sammy flying across the floor onto the pile of broken glass.

Paul reached down and grabbed Sammy's collar, then pressed his face into the glass. 'Admit it!'

Sammy tried to wriggle but he was only cutting his cheeks. 'Admit what?'

'You killed him!'

'I've done nothing!'

A big shard glinted under the spotlight.

Just out of his reach.

Sammy tried to get it, but Paul grabbed his hair and slammed his forehead into the glass. Felt like some went into his eye.

But Sammy managed to grab the shard. He flipped it around and lashed out with it.

The glass jammed into Paul's balls.

Paul screamed, the loudest sound Sammy had ever heard. He clutched his groin and collapsed to his knees. His jeans were already soaking red.

Sammy stabbed him with the glass a few times in the chest, then across his throat.

The shout became a squeal now. Then a damp gurgle.

Paul stumbled around, bouncing off the walls, then staggered into the kitchenette. 'You bast—' He fell over, cracking his head off the cooker.

Sammy lay back on the floor by the couch, glass against his skin.

Still got it.

Still fucking got it.

CHAPTER TWO

DS Callum Taylor was stuck in the back of the police car, back where suspects would usually go. It had that faint reek of urine and sick. No matter how hard they tried to clean it, they could never get rid of the worst. And the suspension was buggered, throwing him around and making his seatbelt engage.

Still dark outside, just some distant lights. Lights they were heading towards.

Castle Gillespie Holiday Park. A faded sign, the jaunty typography and naff illustration dating it back to the Nineties. No sign of a castle and any holiday here would be *miserable*. The caravans were arranged in a grid like giant gravestones.

The car pulled up.

'Let's get you out, Sarge.' PC Jim McIntyre got out of the squad car first, the indicator still flashing, and put on his cap like a good boy. He opened the back door.

'Thanks, Constable.' Taylor got out and was thankful for his thick coat. No matter which way you cut it, the standard Police Scotland uniform was no match for a winter in the Scottish Borders. Especially not down here and up this high, exposed to all the elements. He shivered as he followed McIntyre towards the entrance. 'Place looks grim.'

'Oh aye. Few caravan parks around here. Nice ones like Lilliardsedge over by the main road are split into owners and renters. The owned caravans are lovely there, all individualised with plants and patios and gnomes and so on. The rentals are like wee hotels. This place, mind...' McIntyre scanned around, a bitter look on his face. 'It's a prison.'

'Well, I'm hoping we can get him into prison.'

'Me too.' McIntyre looked over to DC Liam Torrance, just getting out of the car. A loud sneeze rattled out, then a moan that was just as loud, then another sneeze. Finally, he got out into the wind and rain.

No way should that lanky sod be on duty, but what can you do with a negative test?

An old man limped towards them. Silvery hair

down to his shoulders, but bald down to his ears too. The owner of an ask-no-questions kind of place like this, all run down and way off the beaten track, would ask for a warrant, or just be as obstructive as possible. Exactly the sort of place big-city gangsters would take refuge. Edinburgh, Glasgow, Newcastle, you name it. Aye, this wasn't at all dodgy. He tilted his head to the side like a chimp. 'You the police?'

'No, we're wearing these uniforms for a swingers' party in caravan six.' McIntyre smiled at him, trying to show he was on his side. 'This is DS Callum Taylor. DC Liam... Torrance?' While McIntyre seemed experienced, that gave away something about him.

Gillespie narrowed his eyes at him. 'And what does DS Callum Taylor want here?'

Taylor held out a hand but Gillespie just sneered at it. 'Just want to see if—'

Liam sneezed again.

Gillespie stepped even further away. 'Better not be covid!'

Liam was rubbing at his nose. Any brighter and Santa would ask him to guide his sleigh next Christmas. 'Sorry, sir, it's just a stinking cold. Tested negative first thing when I came on shift.' A sharp glare at Taylor. 'Unless I've developed it in the last two hours, it's not covid.'

'Right.' Looked like Gillespie wasn't going to take that as a given. 'Why are you here, gents?'

'Sir, Liam and I are detectives based in Glasgow.'

'Very pleased for you.'

'We're following up some intel that one Paul Templeton is staying here.'

'Doesn't ring any bells.'

'Well, you better get in some better campanologists, because we know he's here.'

'Campan-whats?'

'Campanology is bell ringing.'

'Cheeky bastard.' Gillespie stood up tall and sniffed. 'Well, you can bugger off if you think I'm helping any of you.'

Taylor got between them, but not too close to Liam. Bloody hell, it was *freezing* here. 'Now, unless you want a whole team of sniffer dogs here, you're going to take us to Templeton's caravan.'

'Don't have anyone of that name here.'

'How many guests do you have?'

'None.'

Taylor fixed his gaze on Gillespie. 'You stay here yourself?'

He thumbed back towards the car. 'Got a bed and a coffee machine in the office. All I need.'

Taylor smelled woodsmoke, harsh like the wood

wasn't properly dried. Make him want to cough, but there were already enough covid symptoms. 'So why can I smell smoke?'

'That's...'

'It's not coming from your office. How many guests have you got?'

'Two.'

'Well, take us to the first one, please. The one with a curtains haircut and a Johnny Cash fetish.'

'Right, aye.' Gillespie set off through the decrepit park.

Taylor looked around the place as they walked. 'Just two guests in this whole place?'

'It's January in the Borders, mate. I don't get a lot of custom at this time. Summer or holidays, sure. Had a healthy Christmas, mind.'

Unlike the caravans. The nearby ones seemed run down, only criminals lying low would stay here. No holidaymakers or people who just wanted to live somewhere cheaper.

A cat shot across their path, disappearing into the thick woodland surrounding the park.

If Taylor was in any way superstitious, he'd be back in the car by now.

Gillespie stopped outside a battered old caravan, as dark as the surrounding ones, and knocked on the door.

'Paul? Got some guests for you.'

'Thought you didn't know his name?'

'No surnames. Rule of mine.'

They waited. Liam sniffed. Sneezed. Blew his nose.

Better not be bloody covid. Whole reason Taylor was here was the other big lump of a DC was off with it.

'He is here, aye?'

'Big Paul.' Gillespie nodded. 'Been here a few days now.'

Aye, this was checking out.

Just as likely that Gillespie had spotted the cop car and warned him, making him run.

'Mind if we take a look inside?'

'Not my place to offer that, I'm afraid.' Gillespie flashed a set of rotten teeth. 'I don't have a key and you don't have a warrant.'

Typical.

Liam and McIntyre were looking around the place too, like proper cops.

He looked around and saw thin wisps escaping from a chimney. Someone was here.

Play this cool.

Taylor charged off towards it.

Gillespie was struggling to keep up.

A wee veranda outside, a picnic table bolted onto some rotting decking, piled high with melting snow.

Not that it was the kind of weather to be sitting out in. Wouldn't be for months, and even then — who'd want to sit outside *here*?

Black curtains, but a gap in the middle.

Taylor peered inside.

Ah, crap.

Carnage in there.

Discarded clothes and pizza boxes everywhere, except the sofa. Which had a body lying next to it.

Male, thirties, covered in blood.

Shite.

He spotted another body in the tiny kitchen at the back, slumped against an ancient cooker.

Certainly looked like two corpses, but he couldn't tell which was Templeton. If either.

'Buggeration.' McIntyre was next to him. 'Control, this is serial alpha, requesting medical back-up to Castle Gillespie. Two injured IC1 males. Possibly deceased. Over.'

Taylor put his gloved hand on the door. 'Come on, then. Secure the crime scene!'

McIntyre was keeping Gillespie back at arm's reach.

'Me first, Sarge.' Liam stepped inside the caravan.

Taylor followed him in. The place stank of death, soiled trousers and blood. Spilled vodka too. The stove was still flickering away, but needed a good poking and another log or two.

He could smell something else, something foul. The bodies maybe weren't the freshest.

McIntyre's radio crackled: 'Receiving. Ambulance dispatched from Borders General. Will be about twenty minutes. Over.'

'Thank you. Over.' Liam went over to the kitchen, to check the guy propped up against the cooker. 'Looks like Paul Templeton over here.'

What the hell was that smell? Like gas, but much more agricultural.

McIntyre was staying outside, arms folded across his chest. 'Who's the other one?'

'Other what? Tenant?' Gillespie cupped his hands around a cigarette. 'Sammy. This is his one.'

Taylor stood up tall. 'Do you mind not smoking, sir?'

Liam was coughing his guts up. Great. Just perfect.

'I do mind.' Spark. Spark. 'Free country, so I can do as I like.' Spark.

Some fights just weren't worth fighting.

While Liam was inspecting Templeton, Taylor crouched in front of Sammy. He absolutely reeked of booze. Seeping out of every pore. A vodka bottle lay on the floor in a puddle of broken glass. Red smears on the base, probably not lipstick either. Matching the blood on his face.

And Taylor clocked him – Sammy Irvine.

Well, well, well.

What's that word where you find what you didn't know you were looking for? Serendipity?

Taylor reached over to Sammy's neck and felt for a pulse. Faint, but there. He grabbed his own radio. 'Control, serial alpha here. One of the victims is alive, over.'

Liam turned around, shaking his head and doing a cutting motion across his throat.

'The other's deceased. Over.'

'Noted, over.'

Sammy jerked upright like he'd been prodded by a taser. 'I HAVEN'T TAKEN MY DRUGS!' He looked like he was still asleep, eyes rolling around in his head. Then he blinked a few times. Seemed to come to.

'McIntyre, can you help me?' Taylor took Sammy's arms, holding on to him. 'Sir, are you okay?'

'My drugs.' Sammy put a hand to his forehead. The guy had two massive lumps on his head, like he was growing devil horns. 'Shite. I don't take them anymore.' He touched his chest. 'My heart's fine again.'

'Sir, we're going to get you outside, okay?'

Because this was a crime scene.

And Sammy was a murderer. Or a suspect at the very least.

For a second murder, unconnected to the one Templeton was being investigated for.

'Okay.'

McIntyre took his arm and Taylor helped him walk Sammy outside, where they rested him against the picnic table.

Sammy was frowning at him. 'Do I know you?'

'DS Callum Taylor, and I'm arresting you for the murder of—'

'Here, can you smell that?' McIntyre was sniffing.

Liam shook his head. 'Can't smell anything, mate. This cold's gubbed everything up.' Liam tugged at his beak. 'Head feels like I'm underwater.'

McIntyre was sniffing now. 'What's he burning in that stove? Coke? Heroin?'

Liam reached over to open it and peered in. 'Could be.' He reached for the poker and prodded at the ashes. 'Need to get this down to the lab for analysis.'

Taylor took a long sniff of his own. Not drugs or anything else. 'Gas!' He shot over to the door. 'Liam, get out of there!'

He looked over at him.

Gillespie sparked his lighter again.

The air exploded into flames and threw McIntyre

flying through the air, pushing Taylor back, like a giant's hand swatting him.

Taylor rolled back into the damp grass.

Something landed on them. Something wet and hot.

What was left of DC Liam Torrance.

CHAPTER THREE
A WEEK LATER

Rakesh Siyal drove south, passing through a wood, snow packed up on both sides of the road. Pitch black behind, not even a house light.

Running late.

Well, running late for being early enough to scope out the place so he could be on time.

Buildings passed on the right. A house, with a family crowded around a table eating their breakfast and singing along to something. Then a jet wash, shut for the winter or at least until the snow thawed.

New houses being built opposite, the workers out already, their diggers cutting away under the arc lamps.

A long gap where it was just trees, dusted with

white powder glowing yellow under the fading streetlights.

Galashiels proper started at the twenty sign. Buildings. Houses, flats.

Rakesh got up from his seat and walked down to the front of the bus. The Christmas tree dangling from the rear-view was stinking, not so much pine scent as toilet cleaner. Heater up full, giving a blast of dry air but the bus was still freezing cold.

The driver was muttering away, riding the back end of a slow-moving van, edging out so he could get past. No headlights, just the Morse code pattern of the road markings. He *could* go for it.

The van's brake lights flashed on.

'Crap.' The driver slowed too, pulling back in and giving it some space. He glanced over at Rakesh. 'Twenty miles an hour, pal. Feels like I'm travelling back in time.' The van was edging away from him, must be doing closer to thirty, but the driver stuck to the speed limit.

The road twisted around to the right, passing a shut-down pub. A big park on the left. A wee lad on a bike with a newspaper bag hanging around his shoulders. Kid looked miserable.

The driver jerked the wheel in and pumped the

brakes too hard. Rakesh had to put everything into not toppling over.

The bus pulled in at a stop. 'Here you go, son. Last one before the bus station.' The door hissed open. Engine running, pluming in the air like a thick mist behind.

'Thanks.' Rakesh grabbed the handles on the door and eased down onto the pavement. He skidded and slid a little bit before he regained traction. A deep breath, then he weaved down the hill, over the train line that had been an almost-constant companion since Dalkeith, then he stopped at a roundabout dusted with ice. Careful. He waited for the bus to shoot through, then crossed onto a bridge. Or what felt like a bridge. He wanted to grab his backpack's handles, but he didn't want to fall. He took a left at a grand old hotel that was a mix of offices and flats now, then trudged down a damp street, splashing through slush. Past Farmfoods and Kwik Fit.

And there it was.

Galashiels police station.

Bloody freezing down here. How could it be thirty miles south of Edinburgh, but feel like a thousand north?

And so bloody dark. A few streetlights weren't working, so he couldn't see if there was anyone in the car park. Lights on inside, but the windows were all steamed up.

Felt like someone was scraping their keys up his neck. Then digging them into his armpits. His stomach was bubbling away, floating nervousness up to this chest.

He took a deep breath of burning air and walked into the car park. A car was making a mess of parking in the only space left, a tiny one at the far end, wedging between the station's wall and a squad car, its blue-and-yellow Battenburg livery like some Diwali treat his Hindu school friends would push like street drugs.

He set off across the ice.

His foot slipped. Then slid.

Craaaaap!

He grabbed a post. Didn't go down. Close shave, but he was okay.

Act like a lion in his den.

The cold tickled at his legs and arms, but he was sweating now.

He strolled across the last few steps.

His feet slipped from under him. He grabbed hold of something. Something smacked loud. Crap. He went down, his arse crunching off the tarmac. Pain burnt up his back. Felt like someone had detonated a firework up his bum. He'd jarred something, he just knew it.

And he was holding a wing mirror. Crap.

He planted his feet square on the ground and pushed up with his hands. Standing, finally, but it felt like he'd cracked something. And not just his dignity.

He tried to snap the wing mirror into place, but it wasn't having any of it. Belonged to an old Audi, so hopefully a pool car and not his new boss's pride and joy. He inched towards the front door, taking it slow. Any lions around would annihilate him.

'Excuse me?'

He turned back. A woman was leaning against a Nissan next to the one whose wing mirror he'd destroyed. Arms folded across her chest. Blonde hair hanging either side of her long face. Didn't hide her eyes, which could bite your throat out with just one look. He hadn't seen her, but the cheeky grin on her face showed she'd at least seen him tumble onto his arse. 'You going to take the blame for that?'

Crap.

'Planning on it.' He took it slower as he walked back over to her. He held out his hand. 'Rakesh Siyal.'

Her phone rang and she checked the screen. 'Sorry, Rakesh, but I better take this.' She charged over the ice like she was a snow elf and slipped inside the station. 'Hey. Aye, think so.' She held it open for him.

Rakesh didn't want to go down again, but didn't

want to look like an idiot, so he took it very slow getting back over there, clutching the buggered wing mirror.

The door rattled shut when he was still halfway.

Didn't even get her name.

He got a stab of fear – maybe she was his contact. And she'd seen it. He'd get a nickname.

Slippin' Jimmy.

The Tumbler.

The Fall Guy.

Cops were brutal. It'd stick too.

He kept on walking, taking the steps seconds apart – move, stabilise, wait, move. He got to the door and let out a deep breath, clutching his wing mirror to his chest. He opened the door and entered, less like a lion, more a timid house cat.

The desk sergeant was behind the security glass, eating overnight oats from a pot, his spoon full of creamy, thick liquid stuffed full of fruit. A big dollop landed on his bearded chin. He licked it off with an over-sized tongue then swallowed it down, staring at Rakesh, then took another mouthful.

Rakesh rested the wing mirror on the desktop. 'This came off a car.'

'Right. I'll sort it out.' He looked Rakesh up and down, then let out a beastly sigh. 'Come on, then.' He left the sanctity of his desk and swiped through a security door leading to a long corridor. He charged along it, then opened a door. 'Here you go, son.' He patted Rakesh's arm and winked. 'I'll sort out that wing mirror you clattered off when you slipped.' He walked off, chuckling.

A man was sitting in the room, interviewee-side. Arms folded, face scrunched up, an almighty scar forming on a cheek. Eyes that looked right through you. Nose that pointed towards two different walls, neither of which was the right direction.

Rakesh took the seat opposite. He didn't know what he was here for, but surely it was interviewing this guy? Talk about a baptism of fire. He reached into his backpack for his notebook and the dossier he'd assembled at Tulliallan on dealing with suspects. All the best questions, in the right order.

One
Build rapport.

He looked up and smiled at the guy. 'I'm Rakesh. Rakesh Siyal.'

'Lawyer, aye?'

Rakesh frowned. 'What makes you think that?'

'That's a lawyer's suit.'

Rakesh looked down at it. Maybe he was right. Cost

him a lot of money. Had to be dry-cleaned, not machine washed. Each of the three he had were the same. 'So, what's your name?'

'Sammy Irvine.'

There. A name. That was good. That was the start of rapport.

Sammy leaned forward. 'Where's Davie?'

'Davie?'

The door burst open and the desk sergeant stood there, scratching his head. 'Can I have a word, sir?'

'Sure.' Rakesh grabbed his stuff and stepped out into the corridor. 'What's up?'

'Mind if I take your name?'

He held out his warrant card. 'DS Rakesh Siyal.'

The sergeant sighed. 'That explains it.'

'Explains what?'

'Why Irvine's got two lawyers when most people only need one.' He shook his head. 'Why did you go into the interview room?'

'Thought I was supposed to interview him.'

'Don't you think you'd have been briefed?'

'Oh, right. Well.'

'Why are you here, Sergeant?'

'Told to meet DI Andrea Elliot.'

'Magic.' Shoulders slumped, he charged off down the corridor. 'ANDI!' The sergeant bellowed it out, spraying creamy oats into the air. 'LADDIE HERE FOR YOU!'

A woman was leaning against the wall, staring into her phone. Her hair was short, a fringe hanging just above her eyes, tucked in on the far ear. She looked up with a kind smile.

The sergeant was thumbing at Rakesh.

Her glowing green eyes sliced through him. 'Siyal?'

'Yes, ma'am. DI Elliot?'

'Please, call me Andrea.' She wetted her teeth. 'Well, the guys call me the Ballbuster. And with good reason.'

'I'll settle for Andrea, if that's okay.'

'Suit yourself. Come on in, then.' She swiped through another security door and held it for him, then led through an open-plan office area. Busy, but there didn't seem to be a lot of work going on. A pair of chatting detectives split apart to let her through. 'Sorry for the mess, but this station's an absolute dump. Melrose is being refitted to accommodate the new team, but for now they're based here in this shit hole.' She opened a door at the back and went in first. 'Ah, fantastic.' She picked up a Greggs coffee from the table and tore off the lid, soaking in the aroma.

No offer of a drink for Rakesh. Just a hand pointing at a seat.

'Sorry, but it's okay, ma'am. I'll stand.' His arse gave

a confirmatory throb.

'Sit, sergeant, you've earned the promotion, now enjoy the fruits of your labours.'

Wow. He hadn't expected that.

'Okay.' Rakesh rested his backpack on the desk and took the chair very, very slowly. Pain mushroomed up his back. Aye, it was bloody agony. 'Thank you.'

Elliot sipped coffee. Smelled all smoky. 'Sorry, how rude of me.' She got up and shot over to the door. 'Craig!' She turned back to Rakesh. 'How do you take your coffee?'

'Sorry, I don't.'

'Okay. How do you take your tea?'

'Sorry, ma'am, I...' He shook his head. 'I don't drink anything with caffeine in.'

'What?' Her eyebrows disappeared behind her fringe. She took her seat again. 'Never met a cop who didn't drink tea or coffee.'

'Sorry, I just never got used to it. To the taste.'

'Your parents don't drink it?'

'No.'

'Not *tea*?'

'I've tried it. Tastes like ashes.'

She laughed. 'And coffee?'

'Like burnt toast. Just... Not for me. Sorry.'

'Well, you'll be chaining the tins of WakeyWakey

like the rest of us by the end of the day.'

'Ma'am?' A big lump filled the doorway. Shaved head, fat and muscle straining his suit.

'Get us two cups of water.'

'On it.' He sloped off.

Elliot picked up her coffee and took a drink. 'Okay, so thanks for turning up at short notice, Sergeant. We, uh, lost a detective last week, so we're a bit short-handed and there's a few off with covid, so you're being parachuted in on your first day in Edinburgh, I believe.'

'Happy to help.'

'That's a good attitude.' She took another drink of coffee. 'Sorry, but DCI Pringle's been dealing with the HR side while I manage Operation Fustercluck here, so I haven't had a chance to check out your background. Where are you based?'

'Edinburgh.'

'St Leonards?'

He nodded. 'It's my—'

'Do you know Scott or Ally?'

'I'd need surnames, ma'am.'

'Wait.' Elliot frowned. 'How can you be a detective based there if you don't know them? Everyone knows Scott and Ally?' She took another sip, then paused. 'Aw, shite.' She slapped a hand on her forehead. 'He's done it again, hasn't he?'

'Done what?'

'Given me a diversity hire fresh out of university.'

'Excuse me?'

'Come on, professor. St Andrews? Oxford? Cambridge?'

'I've got a degree from Strathclyde, if you must—'

'A bloody student. He's saddled me with another bloody student.' She was fiddling with her phone. 'How do you become a DS if you're a recent graduate?'

'Sorry, but I'm not.'

'You just told me you're a DS! And a graduate!'

'No, sorry, I'm not a recent graduate. I qualified six years ago.'

'Qualified? In what?'

'Law.'

'A *lawyer*.' She laughed. 'Christ…' She rolled her eyes. 'What's the difference between a lawyer and a field of bulls?'

'Ma'am, I—'

'The lawyer charges more.'

Rakesh smiled. 'Ma'am, I appreciate the—'

'How does a lawyer sleep?' She held his gaze. 'First he lies on one side and then on the other.'

'Ma'am, I appreciate the jokes but—'

'So, you're a direct entry, then?'

Straight for the jugular.

'That's correct, ma'am.'

'Well. I'll try not to hold it against you.' She rested her coffee on the table and brushed the back of her hand across her lips. 'Still don't understand how you don't know Scott.'

'It's my first day.'

'Your *first* day?'

'Well, I spoke to DCI Pringle yesterday and he told me to come here, so —'

'Sod this for a game of soldiers.' She put her phone to her ear and sat there, clicking her tongue. 'Voicemail, great.' She sat back, left hand linking into her right arm. 'Jim, it's Andi. If you're going to screw me, at least do me the honour of some foreplay first. In case you're wondering, I'm not actually talking about foreplay, I'm talking about you saddling me with a bloody new-start direct-entry *lawyer*. Call me back. You hear?' She stabbed her finger against the screen.

'Are you sure you should've left that message?'

'Everyone likes a bit of a joke. You better get used to it.' She glowered at Rakesh. 'Listen, you've come in as a detective sergeant, whereas the rest of us have earned their rank in blood and sweat. Trauma. Seeing stuff. Dealing with things. I've got underwear with more time in the job than you. You went to Strathclyde. Big wow. I got my degree from the university of life. And you know what I got given to me in my career?'

He couldn't hold her gaze. 'No. Sorry, but I—'

'Fuck all. I got given absolutely fuck all. Everything I have, I've earned.'

'That's a bit of a reductive attitude.'

'A what?'

'The police service is a very broad church and we need people with all experiences, and from all backgrounds. You worked your way up from uniform, the hard way, and that's great. But it doesn't give you a complete picture of society, does it?'

She took another drink of coffee and had a foam moustache. She wiped it away, smirking. 'Sergeant, let me be absolutely clear on this. You are on a very short leash. First mistake, first sign of trouble and you're gone.'

He felt himself frowning. 'You think I've missed out by not paying my dues on the street. But I'm a good cop.'

'Aye?'

He was sweating. What a way to make someone feel welcome... 'I've been trained.'

'Training... Okay, so you're like a probationer in a detective sergeant's suit.'

'With all due respect, Tulliallan is—'

'Aye, aye. My point is there's education, which is what you've had, and there's training, which you do on the job. You've been *educated* at Tulliallan, learning from experts. But you haven't been *trained*. I've forgotten more about being a cop than you'll ever know. How they can expect to carve out a detective sergeant in a few lectures, I don't know...'

'I might have a few rough edges, but I make up for it by being polished in other areas.'

'Well, I look forward to seeing that in action.' She sipped her coffee. 'Okay. Let me explain the team structure like I'm reading from a textbook, see if that helps. How much do you know?'

'Well, I had a brief conversation with DCI, eh, on the phone last week.'

'DCI eh. Right. Davenport? Pringle?'

'Not Pringle.'

'Well. Pringle's my boss for the next week or so. Hopefully he explained that there was an incident down here last week. Local lot messed up a murder.'

'You're not local?'

She frowned. 'Eh?'

'You said the local lot messed up. You've got a local accent, though.'

'Right, right. I'm from here originally, but I'm based in Edinburgh now. Sent down here to manage... *this*.

And you're down here too. Think of it like Hell, but colder.' She looked him up and down. 'I don't like you, I don't trust you and I certainly have no respect for you.' She picked up the coffee again. 'And people like you make good cops miss out on decent roles.'

'People like *me*?'

'You don't belong here.'

His mouth hung open. 'Is this a race thing?'

She raised her hands. 'God no! I didn't mean it like that.'

'How did you mean it, then?'

'You as a direct entrant.'

'I'm second-generation Indian, though. Whenever I've heard "people like you", they don't mean Rangers fans or owners of Android phones.'

'It's just a joke, son. Banter.'

Rakesh swallowed it down like a pint of vinegar. 'It felt very much like a—'

'Your accent's Glasgow, right?'

'Hamilton.'

'Ah, should've known. Worked a case there many moons ago. Nasty one.' She wrapped her hands around her coffee cup. 'Are we cool?'

Was he cool with being racially abused and belittled on his first day?

Trouble was banter was a one-way street. He'd

spent his life having to put up with that kind of bullshit. Laughing it off, swallowing it down. Putting it behind him.

Being cool with it.

She was bloody lucky there were no witnesses to hear that.

'Well, I don't think any of what you've said is very politically correct, ma'am…'

'Oh, so you're woke?'

'Woke is a pejorative term that—'

'Listen. You're right. It might not be woke, but fortunately for me, I'm a DI with twenty years' credibility and experience. You have twenty seconds of seniority, the last ten of which you've spent messing yourself in my office. There are ten people out there who'll swear blind they heard every word and none of them will remember anything bad.' She took another foamy sip. 'Now. Are we cool?'

Rakesh nodded. Felt like someone had stomped on his grave. 'We're cool.'

'Excellent.' She got to her feet. 'Well, unfortunately, I've got to attend a meeting down in Hawick, but one of the DSes will show you the ropes. Get you started on some of that on-the-job learning you so desperately need.' Her nostrils twitched. 'But first, go and make sure you haven't literally crapped yourself.'

CHAPTER FOUR

Worst thing was she was right too – he smelled like he'd crapped himself. Everything seemed okay, but he absolutely stank. Must be the smell of fear. And he didn't have any deodorant with him. Crap. He tucked himself back in, grabbed his backpack and left the cubicle.

Whistling came from the other one.

Both sinks were cracked. The left had a massive chunk out of the avocado running from tap to plughole. Probably a huge problem underneath, so he took the right one, turning the tap.

And blasting his face, his shirt, his tie, his suit.

He snatched it off and water dribbled down his face.

He was soaked.

Crap.

The other door opened and a big guy stepped out, frowning at him. He towered over even Rakesh. Must be six foot six. Basketball player height. Well, what passed for it this side of the pond. Gave Rakesh a nod. 'Lawyer?'

He shook his head. 'First day.'

'Well, you're certainly clean.' He chuckled and handed Rakesh some paper towels. 'That tap's a bastard.' His one was the opposite, just a vague dribble.

'Looking for DS Taylor. Know where he's based?'

'Top of the stairs, first right, second left.'

'Cool, thank you.'

'No worries. Hope you dry off; don't want that freezing outside.' He stepped out of the toilet.

Rakesh leaned forward, clutching the edge of the sink. He didn't make eye contact with the damp idiot in the mirror. Instead, he grabbed his backpack, stuck it over both shoulders, and walked off out of the bathroom.

Top of the stairs, first right, second left.

Elliot could've shown him herself. Should've introduced him. But no, she hadn't. Still, he was a big boy. He had this.

Not the first time Rakesh had to put up with this kind of nonsense, either.

Someone had pinned a note to the door:

FALSE START

> The big boys

Scribbled underneath:

> are in the butchers

Rakesh had no idea what it meant. He knocked on the door.

'Come!'

He opened it and popped his head in. A tiny room with four workstations arranged in a grid, all facing the middle. Two men tapped at their laptops with one finger. The one in uniform burped and not into his hand. No apology.

The other two seats were empty – presumably one would be Rakesh's.

The non-burper looked up. Greying hair swept back in a big quiff. Cleft chin with a hole that looked deep enough to hide many secrets. Exhausted eyes, bloodshot and raw.

The guy from the toilets.

He winked. 'Well, you've found DS Callum Taylor.' He got to his feet, towering over Rakesh, and thrust out his hand. 'You must be the new fish, eh?'

'DS Rakesh Siyal.'

'Come on, then, let's grab ourselves a coffee from the canteen.'

'I don't—' He caught himself. Last time hadn't exactly landed well for him. 'Coffee would be great.'

'Good. Word of advice – don't sit with this moron too long. Can feel an IQ point slip away with each passing hour. Right, Pete?'

Pete didn't look up, just winched up his middle finger. 'You started at a very low point, Cal. Never met anyone with negative intelligence until now.'

Taylor winked. 'I love you, man. Like a brother. A brother I'd drown in the bathtub.'

Pete scowled. 'You'd bathe with your brother?'

'When we were kids!'

'Aye, aye.' Pete was laughing. 'Get me an Irn Bru, you big weird bastard.'

Taylor laughed, then patted Rakesh on the shoulder. 'Come on, son.' He barged past him, ducked under the door, then raced along the corridor to the stairs Rakesh had just climbed. At least Taylor held the door for him to catch. 'Pete's alright. Good laugh. Thick as two short planks, but a decent copper. First day, eh?'

'Aye.'

'As a cop, I hear?'

'Right.'

'Don't sweat it. Once you've mastered how to use

taps, interviewing suspects to an agreed strategy will be child's play.'

Great.

This was all going to follow him around.

'I mean, I have been trained.'

'Sure, I get it. I'm just messing. Still, it's a baptism of fire.' Taylor skipped down the steps like a gameshow host. He took the left door at the bottom of the stairs and entered the canteen, a small boxy room smelling of bacon, black pudding and cement. Better than Rakesh's own funk, at least.

A middle-aged woman in a hairnet worked away at a hotplate, singing along to an old Doobie Brothers song on the radio.

A wee guy stood by the coffee machine, his moustache more a cocoa smear than macho hair. 'What can I get you, Callum?'

'Filter for me. And a tin of the orange stuff.' Taylor looked around at Rakesh. 'Coffee?'

'Peppermint tea, if you've got it.'

The server winced. 'Got green tea. That do you?'

Pretty much as far as you could get... 'Decaf?'

'Thought green tea *was* decaffeinated.' The wee man started sifting through a Twinings box.

'I'll take a coffee.'

'Cool.' The server waved over to the window like he

was running a café rather than a manky police canteen. 'I'll bring them over, lads.'

Rakesh took a seat, looking over a river to a car park at the back of an old church. 'Is that the Tweed?'

'Well, geography's the first thing we need to sort out.' Taylor thumbed behind them. 'The Tweed runs south of the town. That's north. And that's the Gala Water, which comes from the north. The rivers meet over by the Gala Fairydean Rovers football stadium. Probably drove past it if you took the A7?'

'I did.'

The bus did...

'Well, there you go.' Taylor sat back, arms folded. 'Okay. Some ground rules here. You and I are the same rank, but we're not doing the same job. No problem with that, so long as you do yours to the best of your abilities.'

'That's my intention.'

'Excellent. I know this is going to be a big culture shock for you. New job, new pressures. Way I hear it, you didn't expect to be based down here, is that right?'

'I was supposed to be on the Edinburgh MIT. DCI Pringle said the team had an immediate opening down here and, well, they couldn't part with anyone else.'

'Cool, cool, cool. And here's the thing... I'm Glasgow, but I've been dragged into this.' Taylor laughed.

'Thank your lucky stars. Guys like you and I, we get to head back once it's all done, but some are stuck here forever.'

Rakesh joined in with the laugh, but he got the feeling he was a million miles away from where he ought to be. From the whole reason for joining up in the first place.

The wee man plonked two cardboard cups on the table and a can of Irn Bru. 'That's on your tab, Cal.'

'Cheers, Bungle.' Taylor tore the lid off one, then frowned. 'Ah, that one's yours.' He slid it over the table.

'Thank you.' Rakesh opened the lid and took a look. Dark, black. No milk. 'It can't be that bad, can it?'

'Green tea? Wouldn't touch it, mate.'

'I meant down here.'

'Right. No, it's fine. Really, it is.' Taylor tipped a sachet of brown sugar in and stirred it. 'My advice? Get your head down, do the work and you'll be fine.'

'That's not really why I'm here.'

'No?'

'I joined the police to make a difference.'

Taylor laughed. 'We all did, buddy. But you'll get used to the fact you're just doing a job, like Bungle over there making coffees for people. You or I can't change the world on our own.'

'No, but I can change someone's world. I can stop them going a certain way, down a certain path.'

'Sounds like you're a bit idealistic. I used up my ounce of compassion in my first year. Well, most of it anyway... a few drops still come out for special occasions. Christmas and my birthday, seeing a puppy in the street.'

'I just want to try to make a difference. That's all.'

'Okay. Well, I'm not going to batter all that idealism out of you, Siyal. That's Andi's job.' Taylor laughed, then took a slug of coffee. 'What's your tragic backstory?'

'My what?'

'Why are you here, Rakesh? Were your parents murdered in a back alley and you've sworn revenge on crime? Were you bitten by a radioactive spider?'

'I... I was a lawyer in Edinburgh. One of my clients died in custody. He was innocent, too.'

'Shite.'

'Right. So I want to stop that kind of thing from happening again.'

'Good luck with your quest, Sir Siyal.' Taylor took a glug of coffee. 'In the meantime, I'll get you doing something useful to keep off Andi's radar.'

Rakesh nodded. 'I want to get my hands dirty.'

'Good. But there's getting your paws mucky and

there's being up to your oxters in shite, which is what this case is all about.' He slurped coffee. 'Okay. Right, I'm not sure how much Andi told you, but we had a wee problem a week ago. Why we're all here.' He sipped coffee. 'Reason you're here too. Someone died. A cop.'

'Seriously?'

Taylor nodded, staring into space. 'DC Liam Torrance. Blown up in the line of duty.' He reached into his jacket pocket and got out a sheet of paper, then unfolded it.

A photo of a white man in his thirties. Stubble, shaved head, nose that hadn't so much been broken as melted and reset so it looked like a turnip.

Rakesh recognised him – the guy from the interview room.

Taylor tapped the face. 'One Samuel "Sammy" Irvine of Govan, Glasgow.'

'I know where Govan is.'

'Colour me impressed, Sinkman. Well, Sammy here was a naughty boy back there. Ran a nightclub called Inner Space. Kind of place you leave your coat by the door but keep your flick knife in your pocket. He's wanted for a murder in Glasgow. Why he fled. Thought he'd got away with it. John McStay. Nasty wee bastard, but still, he didn't deserve thirteen stab wounds to his chest.'

Rakesh took a sip of coffee. Yep. Burnt toast. 'Definitely Sammy?'

'Aye. His DNA's on file for some minor stuff way back when. Fights in clubs, that kind of thing. Got done for it. Year's probation, massive fine, no time inside.'

Rakesh sat back. This sounded like the kind of case where he could make a difference. Someone's life had been ended by Sammy Irvine. Taking him down was going to improve things for the grieving family members. 'So what do we need to do?'

'Found him hiding out in a caravan down by Jedburgh. Unfortunately, it wasn't by us. The trail had grown cold on him and I was actually hunting for Paul Templeton, another Glaswegian scumbag, also staying at the caravan park. Last Monday, we got a lead, turned up there and... Bedlam. Looks like they'd got into a fight over God knows what. Templeton was dead. Irvine alive. Great. Bad news is, the owner managed to ignite the gas tank and blew up his caravan before we could get forensics in there. Or Templeton out of there.' He shut his eyes. 'One of my better lads died too. So there's no direct evidence of Irvine's involvement in that murder now. Caravan park's empty at this time of year, so no witnesses either. Could be someone attacked them both. Who knows.'

'So you need me to get involved in getting evidence against him?'

'Nope. That ship's sailed, I'm afraid.' Taylor took a sip of coffee. 'We can't charge him for that murder, much as we've tried. Had him in here for a week and he's keeping quiet. My lot in Glasgow South can prosecute him for the murder of John McStay, so I need you and Jolene to drive him through to Glasgow.'

'That doesn't sound like a detective's job?'

'Well, it is and it isn't. But we've done a risk assessment of his transfer. Drunken scrap, so he's deemed low risk. Cuffs in the back of the car.' Taylor reached over and clapped his arm. 'Besides, it'll get you away from Elliot for the best part of a day.'

CHAPTER FIVE

Back out in the cold, Rakesh felt the heat dissipate from his cheeks.

Driving a suspect to Glasgow. Exactly what he'd got into the police for...

He poured the rest of his coffee into the frosted plant pot by the entrance, then stuffed the carton into recycling.

'Well done. It'll freeze if you pour it on the ground.'

He turned around.

'And we know you can't handle frozen ground.' The woman from earlier, the one who'd watched him slip and fall right on his arse, tearing off a wing mirror. Her hair was now tied up in a severe ponytail that stretched out her forehead. She strode past him and unlocked a green Audi caked in mud. The car he'd torn the wing mirror off. He couldn't tell which one – whoever had fixed it had done a cracking job. Wasted as a cop. She smiled at him, but it was colder than the air. 'DS Siyal, right?'

'For my sins. Take it you're Jolene?'

She held out a hand. 'DC Archer. Pleased to meet you.'

He shook it. 'And you. But I'm begging of you please don't—'

'Come on. Don't you think I've heard that all my life?'

'Sorry.' Rakesh was blushing. 'Forget it.'

'Mum was a huge Dolly Parton fan.' She smiled. 'So. Do I call you Sarge or what?'

'Rakesh is fine.'

'Nice name.'

'Thanks. It means "Lord of the full moon day".'

'Is it from Pakistan?'

'India.'

'Cool. You want to drive, Sarge?'

He frowned at her. 'What's the protocol? Does the senior rank drive? Are you supposed to drive? Is it elitist if I assert the privilege of rank? Am I being discriminatory or misogynistic if I drive or insist you—'

'Fuck's sake, give me the keys.' She snatched them

out of his hand. 'Doesn't have a satnav, so you're on navigation duty.'

'Doesn't need much, does it? Up the A68 to Edinburgh, then around the City Bypass to the M8. Right?'

'And where's the fun in that? I'd rather go across country. Peebles, Biggar, that kind of deal.'

'Constable, it should be there and back. Quickest route, no messing around.'

'Aye, but it's so much prettier that way.'

She wasn't listening. 'Constable, when and if things go wrong, we have to at least appear to have done the right thing. Okay?'

'So, now you're asserting rank?'

'That's right.'

'Cool.' She got into the driver's seat.

The station's side door clattered open and DS Taylor lumbered out, his meaty fist wrapped around the shoulder of a skinny wee sod. Head bowed, hands cuffed behind him, letting himself be led across the car park to the pool car.

Sammy Irvine.

Tanned in January after staying in a Borders caravan park for the best part of a month. Hard to believe someone that size was capable of murder.

Rakesh opened the back door for him. 'There you go, sir.'

Sammy stared at him. 'What?'

'I'm here to drive you through to Glasgow.'

Sammy stared at him, like this was the first time anyone had ever treated him with respect. 'I didn't do it. Nobody believes me.'

'Sure, I believe you.' Taylor rolled his eyes. 'Thousands wouldn't. Our prisons are filled with the self-proclaimed innocent, so you'll be in good company.' He gripped Sammy's shoulder. 'Watch your head.' He even ducked it before he nudged him in the back of the Audi, then leaned in and secured him. 'There you go.' He dropped a key in Rakesh's hand. 'You touched him last.' He strode off across the car park, whistling the *X-Files* theme tune. 'Glasgow will be expecting you, so chop chop.'

'Aye, you wanker.' Jolene got in the car and stabbed the key in the ignition. 'Ah, buggernuts.'

Rakesh joined her in there. 'What's up?'

'Low on fuel.'

CHAPTER SIX

One of those winter days where the sky was a deep blue. Not even contrails, just emptiness prickled by the last light of stars.

Rakesh hoped it'd stay like that. Any moisture would turn into snow, which would melt and turn into ice. And that'd make it impossible to get back home after his shift.

Listen to him.

A shift. He was a real cop now. Doing real cop stuff. His dream was real.

They passed the turning marked for the Leaderfoot Viaduct, a narrow lane winding downhill. Rakesh had no idea what it was. Roman? Victorian? They shot across the Tweed, glistening in the morning frost, and there it was – a huge bridge spanning the river valley from hill to hill like some giant brick centipede.

And the bloody car really didn't have a satnav. Rakesh sat back and clutched his phone, but really it was just point and click driving up this way. 'You know it doesn't make that much difference how slow you go, right?'

She looked over at him, narrowed her eyes, then around at Sammy. 'What kind of music do you like?'

'What do you care?'

'I care that people are in comfort.'

He was looking out of the window. 'EDM.'

'Electronic dance music. Right.' Jolene turned the stereo on. She reached into the side pocket and slid a CD into the player. The disc whirred, then the speakers burst into life. A guitar strummed, the display read:

Nirvana, *Smells Like Teen Spirit*.

Drums and bass clattered in, loud as if they were in the same room.

Jolene reached over and turned the fader all the way to the back so it was all Sammy would hear. 'Speak quietly. We have a prisoner in the back, after all.'

'Don't you think that's a bit loud?'

'Come on, there's nothing in the Geneva Convention about music. What did you say?'

Kurt Cobain screamed into the chorus.

'I was saying, you're going pretty slowly. It won't make much difference. We're only a couple of miles away and you've got thirty miles of fuel left.'

She spoke in an undertone: 'Don't want to run out, though. We'll *never* hear the end of it if we do.'

'I can imagine.'

'Trust me. You'll go to a station on Shetland or the Outer Hebrides and they'll know you as Petrolhead or something.'

He laughed, but she wasn't joking. Then again, being christened Jolene probably meant her fuse was always really close to the bomb. 'So, are you Edinburgh or Glasgow?'

'Eh? I'm from Perth.'

'No. I mean, you're seconded here from either Edinburgh or Glasgow. Right?'

'No.'

'No?'

She sighed, keeping her eyes on the road. 'No, I'm like you. I'm based down here permanently.'

'Oh. Cool. But I'm Edinburgh.'

She looked over, her eyebrow raised. 'Sure?'

'Right. That's the plan. I'm here to help out. Gather someone died?'

'Right. One of the Glasgow lads. Problem with plans, though, is they have a habit of changing.'

'Can't be that bad?'

She sighed. 'It's shit down here. So boring.'

'Boring doesn't have to be bad.' Rakesh looked on the back seat. 'You okay there?'

In the fug of loud grunge, Sammy wasn't looking out of the window, just stared at his cuffs. His hands were shaking, violently. The kind of tremors you got from alcohol withdrawal.

Rakesh gave him a few seconds, but got nothing.

There was a rancid smell in there, not all of it from Rakesh's BO. Like someone had crapped their pants.

The clicking of the indicators.

He looked back to the front just as they passed the sign for Earlston. A town which seemed to be all outskirts with nothing in the middle. A greasy spoon on the left, then a petrol station in front of a brand-new Co-op.

Jolene left the road and pulled up at a pump. She had the choice of all of them but took the one furthest away. 'You filling this or do you want me to, Sarge?'

Rakesh was the ranking officer here. And he needed to learn how to claim expenses as a police officer. Had to be easier than in his old gig.

She laughed. 'Can you not do anything without overthinking it?'

'Fine. I'll do it. You guard him.' Rakesh got out into

the cold and walked around the car. No fuel cap. Bloody thing was on the other side. He opened it and checked it was actually diesel – won't make *that* mistake again. Sure enough, it was. He got the diesel nozzle and snaked it around the back of the car. Caught it on the wiper, but a tug freed it.

Christ, it was bloody expensive now. Hopefully a tankful would get them to Glasgow and back.

The machine clunked and whirred as it pumped, leaving his gaze free to explore. Ah, the town was over to the right, perpendicular to the main road.

He needed to have a word with Elliot – whoever was in charge of these pool cars needed to do their job and make sure they weren't left empty like this. And didn't smell like that.

The nozzle clicked. He must've zoned out, but the car was full now, so he put the nozzle back.

Jolene got out. 'Laughing boy needs the toilet.'

Rakesh rolled his eyes and let out a deep breath, misting in the cold morning air. 'Can't he wait?'

'He's absolutely stinking in there. Says he's going to shit his pants.'

And nobody, not even a grizzled street veteran, wanted to travel in a car with that. He'd been stinking already, so he definitely needed to go. And Glasgow was two hours away.

'I assume you know all the right stuff to do?'

'I have been trained, yes.' Rakesh grabbed Sammy's wrist and dragged him across the forecourt. He went inside and the bored teenager behind the counter looked up from his phone.

'Police. Need to take a prisoner to the toilet.'

'Sure.' Back to his phone, waving towards the back of the shop.

Rakesh led him through the Co-op, past chillers filled with cheese and cold meat. A couple were having a slight domestic by the pizzas, but shut up as they passed. Hard to tell whose expression was more sour.

Rakesh opened the bathroom door. Just one stall. He nudged the door – empty. He searched it for contraband. Nothing. Clean. Well, as clean as public toilets got. 'Okay, there you go.' He held the door for Sammy. 'This stays open.'

Sammy held up his bound wrists. 'Need you to—'

'You're staying handcuffed.'

'Come on, mate. Are you really going to take my pants down, point Little Sammy at the bowl and then wipe my arse for me?'

Rakesh felt a bead of sweat drip down his forehead. 'No, you're going to do all of that yourself.'

'Not with these bad boys on.' Sammy tilted his head

to the side. 'Come on, you're a big lad. Just give me a wee bit of dignity and I'll not give you a problem.'

Rakesh stared at him. Looked him up and down. Checked the stall again.

Sod it.

Rakesh uncuffed him and let him have his privacy. 'Right, I'm going to pay. I'll be back soon.' He nudged the stall door shut and pretended to close the door back to the shop.

'Man alive.' Sammy grunted and it sounded like he'd dropped thirty-six tins of soup down the pan.

Yeah, he could trust him.

Rakesh opened the door and crossed the shop.

The arguing couple were by the till, the woman grabbing the receipt and giving Rakesh a caring look before wandering off.

'Pump four, aye?'

'Thanks.' Rakesh held up his card.

The kid pointed at the machine. 'When you're ready.'

Rakesh tapped his card against it and looked out of the window.

Jolene was out of the car now, talking on her phone.

Helping a murderer to take a dump was exactly why Rakesh had joined the force...

'Want a receipt, mate?'

'I'm good, thanks.' Rakesh gave a nod, then crossed back towards the toilet. He stopped dead. 'Sorry, I do need that receipt.'

Daft twat.

'Aye, here you go.' The lad slid the paper under the partition.

'Thanks.' Rakesh took it and left him to it.

He caught a flash of movement.

Jolene was waving at him.

He charged outside, the cold air hitting him like a slap.

Jolene was pointing behind him. 'He's run off!'

Rakesh clocked Sammy shooting off through the car park at the back of the Co-op.

Crap.

Sammy jumped over the wall and tumbled over. Then he was up and bombing down a lane running along the back, heading up into the hills.

Blood thudded in Rakesh's ears. A sick feeling in his guts. He'd let a murderer escape on his first day.

No chance they could catch him on foot, but he could in the car.

Rakesh got behind the wheel and hauled on his seatbelt. Key was still in the ignition, at least. The engine growled as it caught and he shot off across the forecourt, cutting in front of a coach as he entered the

A68. Waved behind him, then floored it, clearing sixty, seventy, eighty. Slammed the brakes, squealing around the bend, then foot down and haring off along the single-track lane, hoping nobody was coming this way. Back up to fifty, but hard to get above it on a road like that in these conditions.

Sammy burst out of a farm, running hard up the stone bridge, a single track climbing up and over a stream.

Looking back the way, he spotted Rakesh. He could jump off either side.

Rakesh hit the brakes.

They didn't work.

He slid across a patch of black ice.

Nothing responded. Brakes, accelerator, nothing. Turning the wheel didn't shift his path.

He was heading right for Sammy.

He was going to squash him between the car and the bridge.

Sammy dived out of the way.

The car smashed into the bridge.

Rakesh was thrown forward, the seatbelt biting into his shoulder, and he banged his head on the steering wheel.

Everything went black.

CHAPTER SEVEN

Rakesh perched on the edge of the bed in the back of the ambulance, feeling like the most useless bloody idiot in the world.

He'd let Sammy Irvine go.

A murderer.

A double murderer.

So much for doing good in the world. For changing things for the better.

He'd screwed up, big time.

And he had one job. One simple job. And he'd made a right arse of it.

The paramedic pressed something against his forehead which stung like lemon juice.

Rakesh jerked his head back. 'Ouch.'

'Come on, man.' The paramedic was Australian.

Rakesh hadn't realised that until now. He dabbed something somewhere bloody painful that reeked of disinfectant. Rakesh braced himself for it, but he just taped something down. 'Anyway, it's all fine. You won't need stitches. Now, be a brave little soldier for me and keep this plaster on for three days. Okay?'

'Sure thing.'

'It won't come off in the shower. When it itches, you know it's doing good.'

'Thank you. Am I fit for duty?'

'After what you did to that car?' The paramedic laughed. 'I'm not sure you were fit for duty before the crash.'

'I meant, can I go back to work now?'

'Sure thing. No concussion, just a minor cut with some mild bruising. You'll be right as rain in a couple of days. I mean you might be unemployed, but healthy? Sure.' The paramedic stepped back out of the way. 'On you go, mate.'

'Thank you.' Rakesh got up and eased himself down onto the flagstones, which looked like sheet ice. He didn't trust anything now, so he took it very slowly, each step feeling like it could be the one that sent him flying. Again.

The morning had brightened, with that low sun right in his sight line. That wasn't helping any.

The bridge was an absolute state. The stones on the left side were all dislodged. Two boulders lay on the road, cracking the pavement.

The Audi was even worse, the front all mangled and twisted. The car's engine was still hissing. The radiator, or any number of other parts in the engine he didn't understand. At least it hadn't exploded.

It was a wonder Rakesh hadn't done worse damage to himself.

Jolene was over by another ambulance, shaking her head at a question. No doubt about whose fault it was.

A car pulled up between them and Elliot got out, scowling. She spotted Rakesh and looked like she was going to lamp him, but checked on Jolene. 'How are you doing, missus?'

'Just fine, ma'am.'

'No concussion?'

Jolene touched a hand to her head. 'He didn't get me. I just spotted him running.'

'Good.' Elliot snorted. She looked at Rakesh, then curled her finger towards her.

Rakesh set off across the frozen stones.

'Andrea!' A ruddy-faced man charged over to them. Navy overalls covering a bulging rugby shirt, wellies up to his knees. Hands like JCB claws. 'See what your idiot's done to my bridge!?'

Elliot rested her hands on her hips and smiled wide. 'Come on, John, it's not *your* bridge, is it?'

'No, but my lads use it all the time.'

'And it'll be sorted soon. Okay? The structure's still sound enough to drive over. There's a lad coming out from the council to—'

'The *council*? This bridge has been here three hundred years. It needs a stonemason!'

'The council employ stonemasons. We'll fix it.'

'You better.' John scowled at the road. 'Bloody council are supposed to be stocking up on grit, but this has been a brutal winter.'

'I'll make sure it's done quickly.'

John stared hard at her. 'You do that.'

'I will.' She held his stare. 'How you doing, John?'

'I'm *fine*. Not having the best of times. Flockdown is killing me. If this goes on until March, my birds won't legally be free-range. They'll only pay for barn eggs and it's half the rate. I go to all this trouble to do it the right way and this happens because of the vermin who do it the wrong way. It's killing me, Andrea. Killing.'

Elliot smiled at him. 'Been meaning to call you, but I've been a bit busy. Got any of your birds going spare? My flock's running low.'

'Aye, sure. Always looking to get rid of the old dears.'

'Eight months is hardly old.'

'It is in my game.' John smiled. 'How many? Five, six?'

'Six would be ideal, aye.'

'Excellent. I'll get the lad to bring them around later.' John rubbed his hands and walked off back into his farm.

Elliot watched him go, her smile broadening with each step away. 'Thing about farmers is they're obsessed with the detail, so they're easily distracted. They want money for each field or each bird. Doesn't matter how much or how little. Just one less worry on their shoulders.'

'So you live locally?'

'Lauder. Easy enough to get into Edinburgh and it's close to my mum. Kids love having hens in the garden. Feeding them, finding eggs. Not so much fun when they die, mind.' She clapped her hands together. 'Now. Don't sneak up on people, you midnight creeper.' She grabbed Rakesh's arm and dragged him away. 'What in the name of the bloody shites happened here?'

'Well, I uh... I'm sorry.'

'I don't care about being sorry. What happened?'

'Well, he needed the toilet. And... I took him inside.'

'Cuffed?'

'Aye, but I, uh, let them go.'

'Jesus Christ.'

'He wasn't a risk in there.'

'There. Was. A. FUCKING WINDOW IN THERE!'

'I know. Now. I know now.'

'Then.'

'Then?'

'What happened next, you tube.'

'I drove around. And the, uh, eh, the car, well—' The bead of sweat slid down his nose. '—well, it shunted into the wall.'

'Oh, thank God.'

'Eh?'

'Well, it's the car's fault, not yours. Daft to have some super-advanced self-driving thing that could crash into the wall of its own volition.' Ice dripped out of her glare. 'See, the problem here is you, Shunty.'

He flinched. 'Shunty?'

'You shunted a perfectly good German car into Scottish stonemasonry. You are a tube! So from now on, you'll be known as Shunty. Okay, Shunty?'

Rakesh wanted to explain to her about micro-aggressions and how labels belittled people, but someone like Elliot was so institutionalised she'd call him woke again and really lean into belittling him. She'd been living inside the hierarchy so long that it was all she knew. She'd been maltreated herself, so she passed on the abuse.

Now wasn't the time to complain, or to try and fix any of that. He'd sort it in time. Very slowly.

Rakesh nodded at her. 'Okay, Ballmuncher.'

Everyone stopped. They looked around at them, then looked away.

Even in the frozen Scottish winter, Rakesh expected to see a tumbleweed roll across the lane.

Then hear a pin drop as loud as a nuke.

'It's Ball*buster*, Shunty.'

Rakesh held up his hand. 'I'll take full responsibility for this incident.'

'Damn right you will, Shunty. Jesus Christ, I'm down here to stop this kind of stuff from happening, now it's happening on my watch. It's *our* job to show you locals how this works, not to write off their cars.' She laughed, then shifted her gaze between him and Jolene. 'While he's accepting full responsibility for this calamity, I'm holding it against both of you.'

Jolene nodded slowly. 'Ma'am.'

'Ah, there he is.' Elliot looked over at a flash BMW pulling up. Taylor got out, face like a weekend in Motherwell. She tapped her nose. 'Never trust a cop who drives a flash motor.' She pointed her finger at them in turn. 'Now, while I explain this shitshow to the brass,

DS Taylor will focus on sorting this mess out here. You pair can repay that trashed car by finding Irvine.' She thumbed over at her car, then tossed the keys to Jolene. 'Take that pool car and try not to shunt it off any walls or bridges. And find Sammy fucking Irvine!'

CHAPTER EIGHT

Elliot's pool car stank of cigarettes and mushrooms.

Rakesh didn't know which was worse. Elliot shouldn't have been sneaking smokes while she was driving a shared car.

But the mushrooms...

Was there mould in here?

Rakesh was keeping well under the speed limit as they headed south on the A68. Bare trees on both sides, the trunks and branches dusted with snow. Every few seconds, he felt the wheel lurch to either side, so he had to correct it. And it made him want to drive even slower, almost like his dad.

He needed to keep it careful, he'd already earned

one nickname that day. Play it well and nobody would use it again.

He glanced over at Jolene.

Arms folded across her chest, lips pursed, eyes narrow.

'You okay there?'

She laughed. 'Hardly.'

'Talk to me.'

'You really don't want to know what I'm thinking, Shunty.'

'Please don't call me that.'

'I'll call you whatever I like after *that*. I'm trying to make sergeant this year and you've just put a big black mark against my name.'

His bubble took another big sharp prick from a needle. Soon it'd be burst, with no hope of reforming it.

He thought joining the police would mean—

Who was he kidding?

Cops were people. Just like everyone else, with their own motivations, no matter how strange.

'You let Irvine go, Shunty. You shouldn't have left him on his own! Uncuffed!'

O-kay…

He'd expected to get a lot of this attitude from people like her who resented him getting in at a higher grade, as though the only experience that mattered was in uniform. But expectations and actually living through it were two different things.

And he'd made a mess of things. No two ways about it.

'Look, I know you think I'm not experienced. I get it. As part of my training, I walked the beat in Edinburgh for two weeks, did the full shift pattern. So I know enough of the—'

'Two *weeks?*' She barked out a laugh. 'That's *nothing!*'

'I was going to say that I know enough of the job to appreciate what you'd gain from two, three, four years doing that.'

'Aye, bullshit. The point is, Shunty, you haven't done the time. You don't *know* the job like other cops do.'

'I know you think that, but maybe you should consider why they wanted me as a DS? I have some experiences that the police think are lacking in the current set up. I was a lawyer for years. I know the other side of the coin. How to play cops. How to build rapport with suspects.'

That shut her up. Or at least paused her. Silence was good. Meant she was thinking. 'Still wish you'd left—'

Her ringtone cut off her reply.

She looked at the screen. 'It's McIntyre.'

Before Rakesh could ask who he was, she'd answered it on speaker phone. 'Hey, Jim.'

'Hey you.' His voice was a croak. 'Jolene, I'm begging you to please—'

'Jim. You're better than that.'

'Sorry.' He coughed. Hard. Sounded like a lung came up. 'This covid's a total bastard.'

All he needed to say.

'Listen, Jim, I'm sorry to bother you when you're off sick, but Sammy Irvine's escaped custody.'

'How?'

'Slipped out a toilet window.'

'What? How?'

'Long story.' She sighed and gave Rakesh some side eye. 'How's your head?'

'I'm thinking through all the lines of *Jolene* and I can't think of a joke.'

'That bad, huh?'

'Worse.'

'Anyway.' Jolene ran a hand through her hair. 'We need to know everything that happened when you arrested Sammy.'

'All documented before I tested positive. That Taylor lad took me and this Liam lad out to—' Cough. 'Sod gave me covid. Has Taylor avoided it?'

'Tested twice a day, aye.'

'Sod. Anyway. We turned up. Dead body was Templeton. Also found Sammy.' Cough. 'Unconscious. Helped him out. Idiot owner sparked up. Caravan exploded. Liam... died. Templeton's charred to a crisp. Lost all our evidence. End of.'

'Sounds tough.'

'Right. I was in hospital overnight. Explosion knocked me into Taylor. Handed Sammy over to the detectives. Wouldn't speak last I heard.'

'Any idea where he could've gone?'

'Asking the wrong guy. Taylor would know better than me. He worked the case. Listen, I'm feeling like shite so I need to go lie down. Catch you later, and I will bring in those DVDs.'

'Bye.' Jolene ended the call. 'Okay, hotshot, I hope your specific skills that cops like me and Jim don't have will help us catch this guy.'

'You're being sarcastic.'

'Am I?'

He didn't say anything, just kept driving. 'What DVDs?'

'We're not there yet, Shunty.'

Sod it. 'I think we need to see this caravan.'

'Okay, Sarge.'

'You don't?'

'No, you're the one with the specialist skills and—'

'We're going there now. Can you navigate?'

CHAPTER NINE

Jolene pointed up ahead. 'Next right.'

'Thank you.' Rakesh took the turning, down a country lane, easing the car onto it. One thing country lanes didn't have a lot of was surface grit, so he was taking it very, very slowly now. Black ice would be a nightmare around here.

Jolene sighed again. 'Can you drive any slower?'

'Neither of us wants me to crash two cars in the same day.' Rakesh took a right-angle bend at five miles an hour, then accelerated to fifteen, but even that felt too fast. 'Actually, you might find it funny.'

'Trust me, I won't.'

Rakesh rumbled along the road and slowed to five miles an hour so he could take the turning for Castle Gillespie Holiday Park.

Something was definitely up with this car.

He lost control of the wheel and slid forward. Crap! Spinning the wheel the opposite way, hitting the accelerator.

Bingo.

He got out of the skid, then continued straight on.

Jolene didn't seem to notice.

It wasn't a road so much as worn-in grooves of frozen mud running across bare grass through a gap in the drystone walls. The static caravans ran into the depths of an evergreen wood spreading out to surround the place. A few trees were still hanging against their neighbours, like a giant had spilled a massive box of matches there.

The caravan park was the opposite of a panopticon, where everyone could see into all cells of a prison. Here, nobody could see into anyone else's caravan. They each had absolute privacy.

No wonder it attracted murderers on the run.

Rakesh pulled up in what passed for a car park. More pothole than bare earth. He got out into the bracing wind. Pretty high elevation here, and the trees weren't providing much shelter on the ground. The puddles were all layers of ice.

Jolene was rubbing her hands together. 'This place could not get any more horror movie.'

Hard to disagree with that.

A battered old maroon Range Rover sat over by what Rakesh assumed was the office. It looked like a toilet block, that pale green you used to see everywhere, not the posh shade that replaced it. Rust cascaded down the walls from the drains, though only one of them was hanging horizontally.

Weirdly enough, a pair of modern CCTV cameras prowled the area. Some money was being spent. The giant fence looked recent too, three metres tall plus razor wire and strong gates.

'Come on, then.' Jolene charged over the ice to what passed for a door and knocked. 'Shunty, get your arse over here.'

Rakesh took his time, stepping very carefully. His bum was still sore from his earlier fall, his ego worse from his crash.

Actually, his bum was feeling numb. Must've wrenched it during the crash. It didn't hurt as much as the nickname, though.

The door opened and a man lumbered out. Dark hair streaked with silver, but thin on top, made him look like a bald eagle. A bald eagle wearing a neck brace. 'Sorry, darling, I'm not taking any bookings.' He reached for the door.

Jolene walked up to him, smiling. 'Fred, how are you doing?'

'Morning, love.' He was squinting at her. 'Sorry, didn't see it was you. These cataracts are killing me.' He coughed and seemed to jerk back. 'I'm shit, as it happens. Neck feels like my bollocks and they're a complete disgrace.'

The pebbles behind them rumbled. A car parked next to them. The windscreen was a smeary mess — hard to make anything out.

A woman got out. Small, maybe five one, five two. Tight jeans and a long black coat with a lime-green bobble hat and mittens. Not a cop, Rakesh surmised. She shivered. 'Freezing.' She charged towards them, zipping up her jacket as she walked over. 'Hiya. Kirsten Weir. I work in Police Scotland's forensics unit. Just need to grab some more photos of the caravan.'

'*Again?*' Gillespie shook his head at her, but couldn't get much movement on it due to the neck brace. 'After the last time? You lot blew up a caravan!'

'Well, that wasn't my doing, sir. And that's not strictly true.' Kirsten smiled wider. 'It was your cigarette that led to the—'

'I was blown off my feet! Landed twenty feet away!' He tugged at his neck brace. 'Have to wear this bastard thing for three bloody weeks!'

Rakesh got between them. 'Mr Gillespie, have you seen Sammy Irvine today?'

His eyes disappeared into their sockets. 'You lot arrested him!'

'He escaped custody today.'

'Bloody hell.' Gillespie grinned, full of admiration, soon replaced by a sour look. 'Well, if I see him, I'll tan his arse. Do you hear? He's due me for that bloody caravan.'

Jolene smiled. 'So let's treat this as us doing you a favour, eh?'

'What a scrotum that boy is. I'm sick fed up of telling bastards like you that I haven't seen Sammy Irvine.'

'Sure, Fred.' She smiled at him. 'Thing is, we need to see if said scrotum is still here without your knowledge.'

'You can see how secure this place is.' He pointed back at the gates. 'Nobody's getting in.'

'Sure. It looks sound.' Jolene smiled. 'It's like somewhere from the later seasons of *The Walking Dead*.'

'Stopped watching that when it went shite.'

'But the gates are open right now and someone like Sammy Irvine… You know he's a sneaky one. If *we* can get in, he definitely can.'

Gillespie sighed. 'Fine. Come on, then.' He set off at

a glacial pace, like he'd been frozen by the weather himself.

Kirsten thrust out a hand to Rakesh. 'Hi, I'm Kirsten. Nice to meet you.'

He shook it, smiling. 'DS Rakesh Siyal.'

She smiled, full of warmth. 'Pleasure.'

'No, it's not. Shunty here let a suspect go out of the window, then shunted the pool Audi off a bridge.' Jolene marched off after Gillespie.

Kirsten frowned at him. 'Shunty?'

Rakesh groaned. 'Please, don't. I didn't want a nickname and now I'm saddled with that.'

'Well, they call me Weirdo, so don't sweat it.' Not hard to guess why... 'Who gave you the nickname?'

Rakesh followed Jolene over the frozen ground. 'Ballbuster.'

'Elliot. Right.' Kirsten rolled her eyes at him. 'You don't want to know why she got that name. Anyway, I've worked with her for a few years. I'm down from Edinburgh to help set up a forensics lab in Galashiels.'

'Relocating a ton of officers and setting up a forensics lab down here—'

'It's just going to be a small lab. Most of it'll still be processed up in Edinburgh.'

'This is all because of Irvine, right?'

'Right. Operation fustercluck, they're calling it.'

'Seems a bit much for one guy.'

'Are you kidding me? This was all over the news. Papers, TV, internet. Questions in Holyrood and Westminster asking for the Chief Constable's head. Procurator Fiscal's still a deep shade of purple. Sammy Irvine is getting off with a murder charge because the evidence was blown up.'

'Crap.'

'Aye. And you letting him go…?'

Rakesh walked in silence, his feet getting good purchase on the frigid ground.

'I mean, if you ask me, you and Jo shouldn't have been put in charge of him. Especially not on your first day. That's a hospital pass if ever I heard of one.'

'DS Taylor said they carried out a risk assessment and it was okay.'

'Sure. But you left him unsecured in a toilet.'

'I thought…' Rakesh sighed. He thought he could be a cop. But he was wrong. Tomorrow, instead of catching the bus here, he'd stay in bed.

No, he had to find Sammy Irvine first. Put that right, at least.

Up ahead, Jolene and Gillespie were stopped beside the burnt-out shell of a caravan.

Rakesh waved at it. 'I thought you'd already investigated this place?'

'Right. Precious little to go on from a blown-up caravan.' Kirsten walked between them, then vaulted up to the open door and stepped inside. The steps were a mangled mess twenty feet away. The decking was a pile of half-used firewood.

Jolene followed her.

Rakesh stayed outside looking in. Hard to make any of it out. A three-piece suite, now just a silhouette. A melted TV. Possibly a mirror on the wall. But it could all be just lumps of plastic or wood.

Kirsten returned, lugging a heavy-duty camera. She spoke quietly: 'Reason I'm here.' She rattled the camera. 'One of my new starts left this behind. Fifteen hundred quid's worth and most of that's the lens.' She rested a hand on Rakesh's shoulder and jumped down. 'Anyway, I got this.' She held out an evidence bag. Inside was a lump of black plastic.

Rakesh frowned at it. 'What's that?'

'I *think* it's a phone.'

'Sammy Irvine's?'

'That's what I'll check back at base. Lucky the camera was here for me to photograph it. I'll add it to the catalogue retrospectively.'

'Thought you were supposed to have been through it all thoroughly.'

Kirsten sighed. 'This is the problem with delegation. People lose cameras and miss evidence.'

Jolene hopped down from the caravan. 'Well, he's not in there.'

'Good.' Gillespie looked around at Rakesh. 'You'll bugger off now, aye?'

'Our priority, Fred, is finding Sammy.' Jolene was giving him evil eyes. 'Has he come back here?'

'Don't have to say anything, do I?'

'Of course not. But if he's here, that'd be great for us to know. Fred, is he in any of these caravans?'

'How the hell should I know? And why should I help? You lot blew up my caravan!'

'That's all being settled by my superiors.' Jolene was blushing. 'You know, a kind word from me could speed things up, or drag things on forever. Your call.' She bent over to tie up her shoelaces. 'Quite a lot of caravans to check here. Of course, we wouldn't have to go through every single one—' She got back up again. '—if you could point us to him?'

'What the hell are you smoking, Jolene?' Gillespie dug his fingers into his neck brace and gave it a good scratch. 'I heard on the radio that he escaped from Earlston half an hour ago. It's about fifteen miles away. Unless Sammy Irvine's developed superpowers, it's very unlikely he'd get here.'

'A superpower like having a mate who drives a car?'

'You meaning me, sweet cheeks?'

Jolene grinned. 'Deny it.'

Gillespie glowered at her. 'Fuck off out of here!'

Bollocks to it.

'Let me handle this, Constable.' Rakesh got between them and smiled at Gillespie. 'Sir, I'm DS Rakesh Siyal. We're all sorry about what's happened to your caravan. It'll get repaired, don't you worry. Whether it's on your insurance or ours, it'll be fine.'

'I haven't got any insurance.'

Bloody idiot.

'Okay, well that's unfortunate, but I'll do everything I can to sort it out for you.' He left a pause, long enough to make him think he was noting it down. 'But right now, it's important that we locate Mr Irvine. He's wanted for a murder in Glasgow.'

Gillespie snarled like he'd stood on a Lego brick. 'He's *what?*'

'That's right, sir. He's evaded us for months until we found him here. And now he's at large again, having assaulted a police officer. Anyone who helped us find him would be greatly rewarded.'

'Right.' It was like pound signs flashed in front of Gillespie's eyes. 'Now, don't you think I'm hiding him here.'

'I don't, but I suspect you've got a few shady characters staying here.'

'Excuse me?'

'Place like this. Off the beaten track. Makes me think we should sniff around a bit. See who's here. Who matches up with warrants. I bet that Paul Templeton's just the tip of the iceberg, isn't he?'

Gillespie laughed. 'Nobody here but us chickens.'

'Okay, if you're going to play it that way...' Rakesh nodded at Jolene. 'Keep him here.' He smiled at Kirsten. 'You're welcome to join me. We'll search each one. See what forensic traces we can find. See what you can match to the DNA of murderers and robbers we have on file.' He set off, hands in pockets, trying to act all causal, even though he could slip and fall at any point.

'Hold on a minute.'

Rakesh stopped. Dipped his head, then turned back around to face Gillespie. 'You tell us what you know about Sammy and we'll be on our merry way.'

'Sammy stayed here seven weeks. Place was busy up till just after Christmas. Sammy kept himself to himself all that time. Except for a geezer called Vic Carter, who he started drinking with. But Vic left just before Hogmanay. Think he got a job in Edinburgh. Maybe Galashiels.'

Rakesh nodded at Jolene. 'Could you do a trace on him?'

'Sure thing.' She wandered off, talking into her radio.

Rakesh focused on Gillespie. 'He speak to anyone else?'

'Nope. As usually happens, people clear out after New Year. For a bit, it was just Sammy. Then Paul Templeton turned up, just over a week ago.'

Rakesh didn't believe him at all. That said, the place did seem dead. No signs of life – TV noise, radio blare, laughter, woodsmoke. 'They speak much?'

'Never saw it. Only heard them the day Paul died. Screaming, they were. Absolute racket. Just so happens that some Glasgow copper turned up not long after.'

'You didn't think to call it in?'

'None of my business.'

'Two of your tenants almost kill each other and it's none of your business?'

'What I said.'

Discretion was Gillespie's watchword. His whole business was built around it.

'Sammy ever get any visitors?'

'Never.'

So it was possible Irvine didn't have anyone who knew he was here.

Until Templeton found him. Was that just a chance meeting?

'Did he ever go out?'

'Every Sunday. Be away for a few hours. No idea where he went, before you ask.'

'But?'

'Judging by the clinking, I think he must've gone shopping somewhere to stock up on his vodka. Polish stuff. Judging by his recycling, he got through a bottle a day. Ask me, Sunday morning was the only time he was sober enough to drive.'

So he had a car.

Rakesh scanned the area around the caravan again. No cars. No motorbikes, no vans, no trucks. 'Know where his car is?'

'Sorry, no.'

'Have you taken it?'

'Hardly. Not worth a full tank of petrol, that thing. Even at today's prices.' Gillespie laughed. 'Besides, I haven't seen it since a few days before the, uh, incident.'

'So, the last time you saw it was that Sunday?'

'Right, yeah.' Gillespie tugged at his neck brace. 'Left in it about half eleven, but walked back in a few hours later.'

So he'd been given a lift, most likely.

Could be he'd settled into an alcoholic stupor and a

moment of clarity made him realise his car was too much of an obvious clue.

On the run from the cops, he should've got rid of it somewhere near Motherwell or Hamilton.

But it could be how he'd travelled from Earlston. To wherever he was.

Gillespie twisted around, his back rigid. 'I mean, you can get the bus from the stop a few miles back there. Quick walk, but not if you're carrying as much booze as he was.'

'You know what car he drove?'

'Sorry. Not really a car kind of guy.'

'But you'll have it on your CCTV?'

CHAPTER TEN

Despite it looking like a run-down toilet block, the inside of the office was plush and modern. Light oak furniture. Local photos blown up on canvasses filled the walls. Gillespie was fussing away at a coffee maker, the strong caramel smells wafting over.

A gaming PC filled most of a desk, a black box with garish stripes currently flashing lime green, then cycling through to an acid yellow.

Kirsten was working next to it, fingers dancing across the keys of her laptop. 'Roasting.' She tugged off her hat and a violent pink explosion shot out. Shaved at one side and wild. She tugged away at it until it was in some semblance of a style. Her cheeks were still rosy, a few shades darker than her hair. She tapped at the screen. 'Here we go.'

Rakesh focused on the display.

The footage was paused, showing the front entrance to Castle Gillespie. Wind and rain, before it turned into snow a week ago on Sunday night. A white plastic bag floated down the lane.

Rakesh got out his notebook and turned to the marked page. His first day of real notes. Dated and impeccably handwritten. Even his mum could read it. 'You said he got back about half past four?'

'Correct.' Outside, Gillespie was a grumpy sod but in here, he was the perfect host. He did a la-da-dee as he clinked cups and spoons.

Kirsten shifted the video to that time and let it play. No sign of the carrier bag. Sure enough, at 16:37 a figure walked down the lane, carrying two Ashworth's supermarket bags. The squashed nose was unmistakeable.

Sammy Irvine.

Rakesh got out his phone and searched for the nearest Ashworth's. None in Jedburgh. One in Hawick, one in Kelso, but a giant one at Tweedbank, stuffed between Galashiels and Melrose, near the train line terminus. 'Any of the three work.' He stopped, frowning. 'Wait, no. The bus. If Irvine had come back here on the bus, then there isn't a direct one from Hawick or Kelso.'

'Have to swap at Gala, right?'

'Correct. Not ruling it out, but I think it's far more likely to be the Tweedbank one. The Jedburgh bus stops there.'

'Okay. Good. You're maybe on to something.'

Rakesh smiled. This was real police officer's work here. 'When did he leave, Mr Gillespie?'

No reply.

Rakesh looked over and there was no sign of Gillespie. A horrific sound emitted from the bathroom, followed by a low moan.

Rakesh checked his notebook again. 'Can you wind back to half past eleven?'

'Sure thing.' Kirsten shuffled the video back and let it play. The plastic bag was stuck to a tree on the right. At some point it'd get dislodged and float free.

The office door opened and Jolene came in, stamping her feet and rubbing her arms. 'Freezing out there.' She unbuttoned her coat. 'Can't get hold of Taylor. Suspect he's still out looking for Irvine like us.' She leaned between them. 'What's this?'

Kirsten was skipping forward in ten second increments.

Rakesh let out a sigh. They were getting nowhere.

'You okay there, Shunty?'

'Please.' He turned to Jolene. 'Don't call me that.'

'So-rrreee.'

He turned back and there it was. 11:44. An old Honda Accord left the caravan park. Took the left turning out, the way they'd come in.

Maybe the Tweedbank Ashworth's was on the money.

Didn't explain where the car had gone, though.

Castle Gillespie might be an absolute dump of a place, but this was cutting-edge surveillance equipment and they now had a very good image of the car. If your caravans were occupied by gangsters on the run, surely you'd want to know who was there and where they were going. More importantly, who was coming in. Most would stay where they were, but if anyone was attacked and killed, it'd be very bad for business.

'Jolene, can you run these plates for me?'

She looked over. 'Can't you do them?'

He could. At Tulliallan, he'd scored just shy of one hundred percent in the detective module. 'Don't have a laptop connected to the Police National Computer. And if you could—'

'I know what the PNC stands for, newbie.'

'Children, be quiet...' Kirsten entered the Honda's plates into the system on her laptop. 'Car's not registered to Sammy Irvine. Poor Walter McGill, whoever he is, probably sold it for cash and the documents never got sent.'

'Funny that.' Rakesh could just see it. Cash transaction, no paper trail, just a promise to do it. 'How about running it through the ANPR?'

'You know I'm not a cop, right?' Kirsten laughed. 'I'm supposed to be back at the station, setting up the lab.'

'Okay, but the sooner we—'

'Relax, I'm doing it now. Here we go.'

A lot of results popped up on Kirsten's screen.

Sure enough, there were hits every Sunday around twelve at the A7 cameras just south of Galashiels, then the same around four o'clock coming back.

But no hits north of that.

The toilet flushed and the bathroom door opened. Gillespie edged out backwards, drying his hands on his trousers. 'Who's for coffee?'

'Milk and two, please.' Jolene smiled at Gillespie. 'These two don't want any.'

'Suit yourselves. I make a lovely filter coffee.' More clattering. God knows what he was doing in there.

Jolene was just standing there, staring into space. Mulling over her life choices. She zipped up her coat. 'Let me help you.' She joined him in the kitchen.

'Need to ask you a few questions about this Vic Carter...'

Sammy Irvine's drinking buddy. Good work – a likely assistant.

Kirsten was hammering her thumb off the Control key. 'Okay, so we've got the car, but we lose it in Gala.' She laughed. 'Lose a lot of things here. Like your virginity.'

Rakesh ignored her, trying to process it. 'Have you run the phone number?'

'Phone?'

'Well, you've been searching for him. I assume you've got his phone calls. We can track his location that way.'

'Listen, Jack Bauer, that's not how it works. He has to be using it for us to get a trace. Has to be on.'

'But you have got his phone records from the network?'

'For the phone we found on him, yes.' Kirsten brought up call records and texts. 'He's denied it being his.'

'But assuming it is...' Rakesh scanned the list. 'Same number called every Sunday around noon. That fits his pattern of leaving here once a week, right?'

'That's true.'

'Can you run that?'

'It's not my job to—'

'I know, I know.' He smiled at her. 'Can you run it, please?'

'Right.' She shifted to another screen then tapped the keyboard a few times. 'There we go.' The screen showed a mirror image, just the calls received from that phone. 'This looks like another burner. Pay-as-you-go SIM. No messages, just calls.'

'So, he's meeting some old drug mate?'

'Decent assumption, but I'm not sure you'll be able to answer it without finding it.'

'Right. But you can get the call location history for this other number, right?'

CHAPTER ELEVEN

'I mean, obviously it's drugs.' Jolene pressed the last buzzer. 'So obvious.'

Rakesh looked around the street. Heaving for this time on a Monday morning in January, especially one this cold. Cars drove in both directions, swooshing through the slush, half of them stopping to let the other way flow through the narrow artery between two banks of parking bays. Pedestrians milled around – two elderly couples stopped to chat, laughing in their big coats, hats and scarves, red faces filled with smiles. On a side street, a school-age kid slid down the ice on the pavement.

Jolene started going through the buzzers again, holding each one that bit longer. Then let out a sigh.

'Well, we're not getting anywhere. What do you want to do, *Sarge*?'

Rakesh didn't appreciate the emphasis on his rank. 'Can you check up on the progress uniform are making?'

'Sure.' She got out her radio and turned away from him.

Rakesh inspected his notebook. This was the tenth tenement door they'd tried so far, but only six of the sixty-four flats had answered. Those that did... None had ever spotted Sammy Irvine, and none had called him. And there were tons more to do, not to mention the many side streets running off Scott Street. They needed a lot more than just two of them plus six uniforms. Maybe it was his job to call Elliot and demand more. Especially if this manhunt had so much pressure from on high.

But maybe he was the patsy. The literal fall guy brought in to take the rap for the cock up.

He knew he couldn't think like that, but it was logical.

Wasn't it?

'Sarge?'

He frowned at her. 'How are they doing?'

She was putting her phone away. 'Same as us,

really. Managed twenty-one, eighteen and nineteen flats.'

'Still leaves a lot.'

'It does. What next? Keep going down this way or start on the side streets?'

The two he'd seen both led downhill, away from the main drag. Rakesh didn't know the town's geography yet, so the roads could head towards the centre or could just as easily lead to fields or woodland.

A few shops lurked back along the main street. 'What about the local businesses?'

'They're pretty much all hairdressers.' Jolene rolled her eyes. 'I mean, literally. So they'll have been shut on a Sunday.' Her phone blasted out. She checked it and scowled. 'It's Taylor. Better take it.'

Rakesh didn't like how he was calling her instead of him, but then again he was new and this was a crunch time.

'Take it.' Rakesh left her on the pavement and walked back to the main street. Sure enough, they were all hairdressers. Utopia Hair Design, Curl Up and Dye, Bev's Barbers. One business that wasn't, though – he headed for the corner shop.

Inside, a fat man with a thick beard was holding up a package. 'Just bloody scan it!'

Rakesh started a queue behind him. He could jump

in, flash his card, but it was better to let this play out, otherwise it would just take forever.

The sour-faced woman behind the counter scowled back at him. 'Keep telling you, son, it's not working.' Double denim, faded Marillion T-shirt. 'Told you. Take it to the Post Office on Channel Street.'

'They don't like me in there.'

'Aye, well, I can see why.' She zapped it one more time with her wand and the light went green. 'Well, there you go.' She pressed a button and a receipt printed off. 'Wonders do happen.' She tore it off and handed it to him. 'It'll go on Friday.'

'Friday? But it's only Monday!'

'Well, it's on the system now, so it'll get there as soon as possible.'

'If this is a disaster, I'll be back. Mark my words.' The big guy stormed off out of the shop.

'Sure you will.' She pushed her glasses up her nose, watching him stomp out. 'Arsehole...' She smiled at Rakesh. 'How can I help you, sir?'

'Police.' He reached into his pocket for the print-out and showed her it. 'Wondering if you recognised this guy?'

'I mean, half of my customers look like that.' She took off her glasses and gave it a second look, squinting. 'No, sorry... Wait a minute...' She was clicking her tongue. Then she clicked her fingers and pointed at him. 'Fruit Polos.'

'Fruit Polos?'

'This lad was asking if we still did fruit-flavoured Polo mints. Obviously not mints, but you know what I mean.'

'And?'

'We don't. Haven't done for years. Not sure if they're still a thing. I mean, I asked the owner—'

'No, I meant, was it definitely him?'

'Sure.' She nodded. 'Bought a ton of vape, some scratchcards and a half-bottle of Dunpender single malt.'

A fancy lowland brand. That didn't match up with the supermarket vodka.

'You any idea where he went afterwards?'

'Oh aye. He got into a stretch limo that drove him down to the Savoy in London where he dined with Lady Gaga and Fish, then he stayed at the Ritz and went to the Pizza Express in Woking with Prince Andrew.' She shook her head. 'How the hell am I meant to know that? That time on a Sunday is mental. Kids wanting sweets, dads running in to get something they desperately need for the roast dinner. You name it, it happens.'

Rakesh was blushing. 'Was he on his own?'

'Who?' She frowned. 'Oh, him. Aye. Well, never saw him with anyone.'

'He was in a few times?'

'Most weeks, aye. Cherryade vape and a half-bottle of Dunpender.'

'Okay. Well, that's been helpful.' Rakesh passed her a business card. The first one he'd ever used in anger. 'Call me if something else jogs your memory.'

'Sure thing, pal.' No other customers in there and she looked bored. Didn't have a phone lying around to distract her so she went back to her Daily Record. Rangers were about to sign someone from Juventus, which sounded like absolute bollocks.

Rakesh stepped back out into the cold and searched around for Jolene. Still talking on the phone, walking in a tight circle on the pavements. He got out his own mobile and checked for messages.

None.

Great.

Still be a few weeks or months before he was a fixture, when he was the first person people spoke to. Being the fifth would be a massive improvement on now.

That lead had been a big punt. Acting the cop, getting Kirsten to run the plates and the phone numbers, thinking it'd gift them Irvine's location.

He had to focus on the fact he had inched forward – the data matched reality. Sammy Irvine had been here and he'd been seen. Okay, so they didn't have him, but they had... something.

He set off towards Jolene – if anyone was going to give that update to Taylor, it should be him.

'Son!' The newsagent was out on the doorstep, arms folded. 'Just remembered. One time, just before Christmas, that laddie paid Old Eric's paper bill.'

CHAPTER TWELVE

The squad car pulled up and a big uniformed constable got out onto the pavement. The one who Elliot had instructed to get coffee earlier. 'Jolene.' He frowned at Rakesh. 'Sorry, don't know your name?'

'DS Rakesh Siyal.'

'Oh, okay. Craig Paton, at your service.'

'Thanks for coming.' Jolene patted his arm. 'How's the search going?'

'Same as you two. Drawing a blank.'

Rakesh frowned at him. 'You were just doing it on your own?'

'No, I had the ghost of Sir Walter Scott helping me.' Craig rolled his eyes. 'Of course I was on my own. Not sure where you're used to, pal, but we're a wee bit understaffed down here. Especially with Macca and Jonjo both out with covid. And what happened to Liam...' He looked around, rubbing at his eyes. 'Okay, so where do you want me?'

'Right, well, can you just follow us up, Constable.' Rakesh nudged the door open, thankful the entry system was broken, then led them up the stairs.

Old Eric just had to live on the top floor, didn't he?

Rakesh trudged up, each step drawing another deep breath from him. Such a loser. He'd just backed down when Craig challenged him. Didn't want to own to this being his first day, did he? Too proud, like his mother always said about him.

Too proud by far.

Rakesh reached the top-floor landing and stepped aside, breathing hard. 'If you wouldn't mind?'

'Not sure why I'm supposed to be the one to do this, but hey ho.' Craig rapped his knuckles on the door.

'Because Sammy Irvine might be inside, Constable.'

'Right, aye, but why—'

The door creaked open and an old man stood there. Teddy-boy haircut, silver moustache, pot belly, brown Fred Perry. Hell of a snarl on him, chewing on a Bourbon biscuit. 'What?' Nasty eyes brushed across each of them. 'Filth, eh?'

'Police, sir.' Craig smiled at him. 'Looking for an Eric Mitchell.'

'You've found him, eh?' Eric slurped from a chipped teacup then popped the second half of his Bourbon in his mouth. 'What's up?' Chewed through the words, then slurped more tea.

'Looking for a Samuel Irvine, AKA Sammy Irvine.'

'Nope.' Eric nudged the door shut.

Craig stepped in, wedging his foot against it. 'Mind if we have a look around to confirm that?'

'I do, aye.'

'That because he's here?'

'What, no! Course he's not!'

This was a side of the coin Rakesh hadn't seen before. How the police gained entry somewhere they weren't wanted. Most of his previous interactions, the police had been in the wrong. All he had to go on was TV shows and books.

Now, though, he could see that his black and white was as many shades of grey as there were grains of sand in the Sahara.

And they needed to gain access to where they weren't wanted.

Craig folded his arms. 'Fine. I'll just wait here.'

'Eh?' Eric sipped from his tea. 'You can't do that. My heating bill's through the roof as it is!'

'Well, if you leave, I'll follow you. If anyone comes here, I'll—'

'This is about Sammy?'

'Right. That's what I said.'

Eric drank tea with a grimace, then set the cup down on a sideboard. 'Know him, sure. He came here a few weeks back when I had covid. Paid my paper bill for me. Gave me a wee drop of my favourite whisky. Helped in my hot toddies.'

'That's it?'

'Sure. There's nothing else.'

'You have any idea where he might be?'

'Well, I know he's got a mate in Lauder.'

'You know this guy's name?'

Eric paused, frowning. 'Keith something. Maybe Moncur?'

'Thank you, sir.' Craig smiled at him then pulled his foot away from the door. 'Have a good day now.'

Eric grunted, then shut the door.

Jolene was nodding at Craig. 'Lauder's just up the road from Earlston. Few miles along the Langshaw road and you're there.'

'I'll get an address for this Keith Moncur.' Craig set off down the stairs.

A sound rumbled inside, deep and bassy. Rakesh pressed his ear against the door.

'You've only just got here, son!'

A long pause.

'Come on. That's not fair!'

Was Eric on the phone to Irvine?

Was Irvine in there with him?

Rakesh waved at Jolene to get her attention, then put a finger to his lips and pointed down the stairs, mouthing: 'Get Craig.' Ear back to the door.

'—not fair, though.' Pause. 'Look, if you bugger off, the heat won't die down, will it? It'll just get worse.' Another pause. 'Well, if you insist. But I'm not ha—'

Craig stepped up to the top, his radio sparking noise. 'What's up?'

Rakesh put his finger to his lips again, then thumbed at the door, whispering: 'Can you get us inside?'

Craig winced. 'Seriously?'

'Either he's on the phone to Irvine or he's there with him. Listen.'

Craig put his ear to the door for a few seconds then shook his head. 'Nobody there.'

'Listen to—'

'Can't hear anything!'

'Jolene, can you run a trace on Eric's landline?'

'On it.' She dashed off down the stairs.

'Shite on toast.' Craig stepped back, then launched his shoulder at the door, cracking it just below the Yale.

It flew open and he stormed inside.

Eric stood there, phone to his ear, teacup pressed to his lips. He dropped it and it shattered, splashing tea and shards of crockery over the lino. Eric's eyes bulged like he was having a heart attack.

Craig leapt into action, grabbing him and cuffing him. He held Eric's right arm and started searching him. 'What's this?'

'Sexual assault.'

'You would know.' Craig snatched Eric's ancient phone out of his hand. On second inspection, it was only the style that was twenty years old – the actual mobile was brand new, barely a scratch on it.

Rakesh pulled out an evidence bag. 'Get Kirsten Weir to process it.'

'Sure thing.' Craig popped it in the bag.

Rakesh stared at Eric, but he wouldn't look at him. 'Are you going to tell me where he is?'

'Don't know who you're talking about.'

'Sammy Irvine.'

'No idea why you'd think that he'd be here.'

Rakesh clenched his jaw, then looked at Craig. 'Take him to the station. Let him stew.'

'Come on.' Craig led Eric out of the flat.

FALSE START

Leaving Rakesh alone in there. He scanned around the poky wee room. Kitchen lining one wall, yellow units about forty years past their best. Cooker with eye-level grill. Bottle green three-piece suite crammed into the rest of it, a coffee table lying between them. A pint glass acted like an ashtray, the butts sticking up on top like a Jenga tower. Eric was too lazy to empty it. Or maybe that was just today's — the room stank of smoke and had that thin haze. A brown envelope lay next to a half-empty bottle of Dunpender.

Rakesh reached for it, then stopped. He snapped on a pair of blue nitrile gloves. Almost forgot. Twat. He tipped out the contents onto the table.

A navy passport and a plane ticket.

One-way flight from Newcastle to Ankara, Turkey.

The passport had the name of Samir Erdoğan.

Obviously fake — using a different form of Sammy and the president of Turkey's surname.

But it was Sammy Irvine's photo.

CHAPTER THIRTEEN

Rakesh had seen it on TV so many times, the cop ducking the cuffed suspect's head as he helped him in the back of the car. And he'd heard so many stories from clients about how they didn't quite clear the top of the door frame, getting a clunk on the head for their trouble. That little bruise under the hair was a constant reminder of who held the power in the situation. A micro-aggression to assert dominance.

So he was mindful of making sure Eric Mitchell's head was a few centimetres lower than the top of the door frame as he helped him in the back of the stinking pool car. Eric wasn't cuffed and he didn't make eye contact with him as he buckled him, just sat there, staring at his feet. Big white Hi-Tec basketball boots. So shiny they had to be new – Rakesh was surprised were even still made. He checked the belt was in place then opened the driver's door, but didn't get in.

Jolene was looking at him over the top of the car, but didn't say anything. Phone to her ear.

'You okay there, Constable?'

'I'm—' She smiled. 'Never mind.'

'Whatever it is, you can say it.'

She looked up at the flat. 'Are you sure arresting an old man is the right thing to do?'

'We've not arrested anyone. Given he's not talking up there, he's just coming in to answer some questions. Standard stuff.' He left a pause, but she didn't fill it. 'Are you getting anywhere with the phone trace?'

She shook her head. 'Landline was disconnected a year ago.'

'What about the burner?'

'Craig's run back to the station to pass it to Kirsten.'

'So we're unlikely to get anything from it?'

'That's right.'

Rakesh leaned into the car. 'You okay back there?'

He got a brief flash of eye contact from Eric, but that was it.

Rakesh waited for it to come back then held the eye contact. 'Do you want me to get you a lawyer?'

'Please.'

Jolene leaned in. 'Absolute leeches. Hate them.'

'They're not all bad.'

'No, they are. To a man, woman and child.'

Rakesh felt the blood burning in his veins. 'You know I was a lawyer before I signed up, right?'

'What?'

'Criminal defence, but with a human rights angle.'

She was nodding. 'Makes sense, actually. Join the police to make a mess of high-profile investigations like this to let scumbags walk free, right?'

'Hardly.' Jesus, where did she get that kind of nonsense from? 'My clients were Legal Aid, but they weren't gangsters like Sammy Irvine.'

'Who were they, then? Murderers? Rapists?'

'A lot of women in difficult situations. Immigrants from all over. A lot of Eastern Europeans. Some Asians like myself. LGBTQIA+ too.'

'I'm sure there's a new letter each week.' She laughed, but the joke didn't land with Rakesh. 'So you were a woke lawyer?'

'That's a bit of a loaded term, don't you think?'

'What, *lawyer*?'

'No, woke. It rhymes with joke for a reason, to belittle and trivialise the quest for social justice. It's used by racists and those on the far right to imply there's something wrong with wanting to make the world a better place for those living on the margins.'

'Right. Sure. Still, I don't get why knowing which pronouns to use would help you be a good cop.'

'I'm here to make things better for people. That's it.'

'Totalling a car is helping people?'

'We botched that and it's on me. But it's up to us to find Sammy Irvine and get him through to Glasgow to face prosecution.' Rakesh pointed inside the car. 'The sooner we speak to Eric here, the better. So please, can you arrange for a lawyer?'

Jolene sighed. 'I'll get onto that now.' She walked off down the cold street, phone to her ear.

The low sun was at the perfect angle to be blinding.

Rakesh got in the car and slid the key into the ignition. He didn't turn it, just let his hands flop down onto his lap. Absolutely freezing in there, worse than outside. A wave of fatigue hit him – day one and he was already knackered before lunch. 'The passport looks great.'

'What passport?'

Rakesh reached into his pocket for the evidence bag. 'This one. You do that for Sammy?'

'No idea what you're talking about.'

'That's his photo in there, right? But it's not his name.'

'Never seen that in my life.' Eric wiped sweat off his forehead. 'Nothing to do with me.'

'Flight from Newcastle to Turkey with the same name too. Looks like someone's on the run.'

'News to me, son.'

Jolene got in the passenger seat. 'Drive.'

Rakesh twisted the key. 'Drive?'

'Kirsten's run that burner and got a lock on Sammy. He's on Channel Street.'

'Where is—'

'Just drive!'

So he did, twisting the key and sparking the sleeping car into life. 'You need to—'

'Turn right here!'

A street of tenements curved around a bend, then eased down towards a long row of upmarket shops and cafés opposite some public gardens. Like a tiny version of Princes Street in Edinburgh.

'Left.' Jolene had her phone still to her ear. 'Aye, Craig, if you could get them to approach from the cinema end, that'd be grand.'

Rakesh took the left, but it was the only option – he'd entered the one-way system. He had a clear run at it and the road bent around to the right at the end, past a Chinese and a sit-in chip shop. He had to stop at the red light. 'Where to now?'

'Wait here.' Jolene opened her door and got out.

'I can't!'

But she was gone, running over the crossing towards a pedestrianised shopping precinct.

Those zigzags on both sides meant you couldn't park there. Not even the police.

Rakesh eased the car through the lights, then parked on the double yellows next to a parking bay. Hazards on.

A modern building sat opposite. Looked like a child in a sheet pretending to be a ghost, arms raised out on either side.

'That's the Great Tapestry of Scotland in there, son.'

Eric was talking.

Rakesh needed to keep him doing that. 'And what's that?'

'A huge tapestry, son. Tales of the lives of normal Scots. Not loads of shite about kings and queens. Real people. Quite a braw thing, makes you proud it's in our town, you know?'

'You've been there?'

'Been there? I helped build it. I'm a brickie by trade, but I can do a few others. Last job I'll ever do, that, but I'm okay with that. Nice to leave a lasting mark on the town.'

Rakesh turned around and smiled at him. 'What was Sammy's plan?'

'Told you, son. Haven't heard from him in ages.'

He was talking about him, though. That was good. 'Why were those documents in your flat, Eric?'

'I've never seen them before in my puff.'

'I don't believe you. You could say he's just using you as a post box, but we both know that's not true.'

Fire flashed in Eric's eyes. 'What do you know?'

'Well, a few things, actually. About what your friend's supposed to have done. He killed someone.'

Eric let out a sigh like a deflating balloon. 'That's complete bollocks.'

'Aye?'

'Aye. Look, Sammy told me all about it. Told me he didn't kill that boy. And I believe him.'

Rakesh looked along the street, but there was no sign of Jolene or any other cops. 'If he didn't kill him, why is he running away?'

'He isn't. Just... Prison, you know?'

'Can't do the time?' Rakesh held his gaze for a few long seconds. 'Nobody can hack prison, not really. It affects everyone. Even the ones that think they can hack it, it changes them.'

Eric sat back in his seat. 'What do you know about it? Been inside yourself?'

'No. Saw it in my old job.'

'Prison guard?'

'Human rights lawyer.'

'Really?'

'Represented a fair few people who were inside. Visited prison a lot to speak to them about their appeals. Thing is, most of my clients were innocent. Some weren't, but the ratio was crazy. I was trying to get the innocent ones out of there. But it wasn't enough. My workload kept going up, but not as quickly as the ratio of innocent to guilty.'

'You're talking about cops framing people, right?'

'Various reasons.' Rakesh swung around. 'Eric, why is Sammy going to Turkey?'

'I've no idea, son. None.'

'Is he running because he's innocent or because he's guilty?'

'He hasn't killed anybody. I do know that.'

'Listen, I know a bit about Türkiye.' Rakesh used the preferred native pronunciation to see if that curried any favour with Eric. 'Represented a few people from that part of the world. For a few hundred quid, you can get to the Turkish border with Syria, then you can just cross over on foot. Sure, it's still a warzone, but you can disappear off anyone's radar back here.'

Eric sat back, arms folded. 'Take your word for it.'

'Thing I don't get is, he was supposed to be hiding out down here because the police were after him. Right?'

'So you say.'

'But he came to visit you a few times. You must be close. You work with him or something?'

Eric sighed. 'I'm his granddad.'

Well, well. That wasn't on the file.

'I'm assuming that's on his mother's side?'

'Leave her out of it.' Eric was nibbling at short fingernails. 'But aye.'

'I know you might not believe me, Eric, but if your grandson's truly innocent, I really want to help him.'

Eric leaned forward, scratching at his thin hair. 'You wouldn't believe me.'

'Of course I would.'

'How can I possibly know that?'

'Haven't you listened to a word I've been saying? I'm not your average cop. I'm not some bully trying to meet statistics. I'm trying to do the right thing here. You give me proof he didn't commit that murder in Glasgow, then of course I'll believe you, and I'll push to get it all overturned.'

'Sure. Right. Of course.'

'I mean it.'

Eric stared out of the window. 'Okay. Sure. Right.'

Rakesh looked for any sign of Jolene, but the street was quiet, just a woman wheeling around on the pavement, her free hand spinning as she talked on her phone. 'I heard you on the phone to him. I know you've been in touch with him for months. Help me to help you.'

Eric sighed. 'Right, here's the truth. Make of it what you will. Sammy told me he was accused of murdering someone. But he also sweared he didn't do it.'

'That's it?'

'No, son, it's not. He told me someone's trying to stitch him up.'

'Stitch him up? You mean a cop?'

'That's what he said.'

'You got any proof of that?'

Eric sniffed. 'Nope. Sammy does, though.' He shut his eyes. 'Way he explained to me... He was hiding out in that caravan park until he got the passport through the post. Mate of his was sending it to me by courier. But it was late, wasn't it? A week ago, Sammy turned up on Sunday, like he always did. Passport had still not turned up and he's losing his mind, son. He's just sold his car for cash. Bought some Turkish Lira with it, enough to get him where he wanted, if he needed to go. He was asking me to drive him to Newcastle, then he was going to fly home, where he'd stay. See out his days over there. If he needed to run, like you say, he could go to Syria. Packet finally turned up last week. But I haven't heard from him since last Sunday.'

'He's been in police custody, that's why.'

'Right.'

'Until he escaped today. And he called you, didn't he?'

'I...'

'Come on, Eric. I heard it. We've got the call record. My colleagues are out trying to find him now. What did he say?'

'Just that he had to get that packet so he could go home.'

And something was fizzing around Rakesh's brain. 'Did you say "home"?'

Eric blew air up his face. 'I did. Why?'

'Türkiye is his homeland? I thought he's from Glasgow?'

'He was born over there. His dad's a Turk.'

Rakesh got out his notebook and flipped through to the biographical information he'd captured. 'Mother is Karen Mitchell. Born in Galashiels, moved to Glasgow. Married Douglas Irvine, his father.'

'Aye, but Dougie's his stepfather.'

'What?'

'Dougie was Karen's second husband. When she was a student, at university in Stirling, she went to Turkey on holiday with the girls. Met this boy called Hakkan working in a beach bar. Fell in love with him. Stayed over there a couple of years, doing the same thing, working bars and clubs. Soon, my grandson was born. Wee Sammy. They moved back here, but Hakkan didn't settle in Gala. His cousin worked through in Glasgow, so Karen moved there with him and Hakkan got a job in a mailroom. Didn't like that either, so he started driving a taxi. Few years later, he died in a crash on the Erskine Bridge. Him and the passenger, both dead on impact. Bang. Goodnight, Vienna. Bloody motorbike. He got off with a broken leg, would you believe? Took my girl years to get over it, but she eventually met Dougie and remarried. Samir changed his surname. He'd already become Sammy to fit in at school.'

'Samir Erdoğan. So the name on the passport's his birth name?'

'Right. Erdoğan means Brave Warrior. Some say hawk. Sammy's skin's quite light and he can pass for a local.'

Jesus Christ.

No wonder Sammy Irvine had been desperate to run. All that trauma in his life. Trying to fit in when your face didn't – aye, Rakesh knew precisely how that felt. So did his many, many former clients.

He fixed a solid stare at Eric. 'I want to help Sammy. Tell me what happened in Glasgow. All of it. I want to know, then I can try to fix this.'

'My lad runs a nightclub. You probably know that. Makes a lot of money, but the police, the council, they all want rid of him. The murder charge is trumped up to do that.'

Sounded like bullshit.

'Right, but that doesn't answer my question. He's accused of murdering someone. You're saying he didn't do it. How can I prove it?'

Eric leaned forward. 'Might want to have a wee word with Callum Taylor.'

'What?'

'Sammy told me he's the one framing him.'

'Why does he think that?'

'Because someone found Sammy, right? Tried to kill him. Nobody knew where he was. Nobody. He was bloody careful, my lad. Really careful. But Callum Taylor leaked some intel on his location.'

'Has he got any proof of this?'

'He does.'

'Can you share it with me?' But Eric was looking away now.

The passenger door opened and Jolene got in, panting hard. 'Sorry, been up and down that bloody street and there's no sign of Sammy.'

Eric sat back in his seat, looking out of the window. Arms folded. Saying nothing.

Still, if he was telling the truth, if Callum Taylor was framing Sammy Irvine, then Rakesh had to help.

CHAPTER FOURTEEN

Rakesh powered up the stairs, heart thumping. He checked his phone, but Elliot still hadn't responded to his texts or missed phone call.

Eric alleging Taylor was framing Sammy Irvine for murder... It sounded nuts.

Equally, Rakesh couldn't let an innocent man go to prison for a murder he didn't commit.

It was why he'd joined the police service. To prevent this kind of thing from happening. To shine a light on it.

He needed more evidence than a grandfather's wild allusion.

Where should he start?

Well. Taylor had been there when the caravan had

exploded. If there was anything, any trace of a lead, it'd be there.

Sammy thought Taylor had leaked his location. Instead of arresting him, he'd sent Paul Templeton there.

That was it.

That was where to start.

Right.

Let's do this.

Deep breath.

Rakesh opened the sergeants' office door and stepped in like he belonged there, like he was a real cop. The smell of Thai curry and rotten banana lingered on the air. Animals.

The uniform guy was in there, head down, working away. Didn't look up.

No sign of Taylor. Okay.

Rakesh sat down and unlocked his machine. His own desk, in the sergeants' room of a police station. 'Afternoon.'

His new colleague looked up now. 'Aye.' Then back at his machine, muttering under his breath.

Rakesh couldn't tell if it was about him.

The sickly reek of an open yoghurt pot congealing in the bin.

Took him three goes to remember his password, but he finally got in.

He could send Elliot an email, raising a concern. Establish an audit trail. Stress how urgent it was.

He could contact Professional Standards.

Christ, no. He didn't have enough yet. Didn't have anything.

His tendency to overreact, to get overexcited by the slightest thing...

Whatever – he needed to give Sammy Irvine a fair crack of the whip.

Samir Erdoğan.

If that was all true, if he was innocent...

Of course Rakesh needed to investigate.

The other guy was on his feet, hands scouring pockets and jangling change. Was his name Pete? 'Get you anything from downstairs?'

Rakesh smiled at him and made eye contact with dull blue irises. 'I'm good, thanks.'

'Cool.' The door shut.

Rakesh's email inbox had three messages.

An internal comms thing he'd glance at later.

A welcome message from DCI James Pringle, which was nice of him.

The third was from Kirsten Weir, the text in the same colour as her hair:

Don't know your phone number, so come and see me when you get this. Two doors down.

Love,

Weirdo x

Rakesh got up and shot over to the door, then realised he hadn't locked his machine – last time he'd done that in his old job, someone had turned his screen upside down. He had to search on his phone how to fix it. He locked it, then went out into the corridor. Did she mean two doors on the left or the right? Sod it, he tried the right.

Right enough, Kirsten was in there.

Not so much a lab as a room full of boxes and some equipment precariously placed on tables. She looked over at him, frowning. 'Got my message, then?'

Rakesh ran a hand through his hair. 'Aye, what's up?'

'You okay there, Shunty?'

'I'm fine. Weirdo.'

'Are you, though?'

Rakesh couldn't trust her with the allegation yet. Sure, she'd been really helpful at the caravan park, but this was super-crucial. He gave her a warm smile. 'I'm fine. Seriously.'

'Well.' She slapped a document down on the desk in front of him. 'Have a look at this bad boy.'

He picked it up and skimmed the cover. 'Is this right?'

'No, I'm in the habit of just making up any old rubbish.' She sat next to him. 'Aye, it's right.'

'So that passport is real?'

'Correct.'

'It's not forged?'

'Nope. Came from the Passport Office in Glasgow. He was born Samir Erdoğan, but he legally changed his name to Irvine. Thing is, you can use the original birth certificate to get a passport, right?'

'I suppose.'

'That's what he's done here.'

Things were stacking up, then. Sammy Irvine was the fiction, Samir Erdoğan the reality.

And running back to Turkey – or Türkiye – might not be the actions of a guilty man, but those of an innocent one who nobody believed.

Why would Taylor frame him?

Rakesh didn't get it.

He could head downstairs and speak to Eric again, but Jolene was doing that with big Craig sitting next to her. 'Take it there's no update on his burner location?'

'Oh no, we've got it.'

'Where?'

'Uniform found it in a bin opposite the cinema.'

'There's a cinema in Galashiels?'

'Good one too.'

So they'd almost caught him.

Rakesh didn't know whether to laugh or cry.

She was frowning. 'What's up?'

'Wondering if you can help me puzzle something out.'

'Sure thing, Shunty. Fire away.'

Rakesh grimaced at the use of the name. 'First, how would he get from Earlston to Galashiels?'

'It's not far. Couple of hours walking?'

'Mm. Surely people would've spotted a guy in a red puffer jacket?'

'Could've cut through any of the timber plantations up there.'

Rakesh looked out of the window up at the hills surrounding the town. The biggest one had a serious forestry operation going on, cutting through the thick green, even at this time of year. The side he'd lost Sammy was similar, but the woods were still untouched.

Kirsten yawned into her fist. 'Besides, it's five minutes in the car, even going the back way.'

That would make sense. But who drove him? Not Taylor, that's for sure.

She reached over for a can of lavender and cola WakeyWakey energy drink. 'What's the other thing?'

'The other thing?'

'You said "first" about how he got from Earlston to Gala. Is there a second to go with it?'

Aye, there was. And it was…

Sod it.

Rakesh looked over at her. 'Listen, you know DS Taylor, right?'

'Right, and?'

'Well. We picked up Irvine's grandfather. Eric Mitchell. He told me Taylor's framing his grandson.'

She laughed. 'Good one.'

'I'm serious.'

She frowned. 'What? You *believe* him?'

'Thing is, I want to investigate it. It's not like it all stacks up. I haven't been through the case files, but…' Rakesh sat back, sighing.

He felt the weight of the allegation pulling down on his shoulders.

First day on the job and someone accused an experienced officer of framing someone for murder.

But the weight that Sammy was innocent was just as heavy.

'It might fit. And I think we should look into it.'

Kirsten was still frowning. 'Have you got any evidence?'

'Well, not yet.'

'Okay. So if you haven't got that, you've got opinion. And they're like bums. Everyone's got them and they all stink.'

'So you're telling me I should drop it?'

'No, but...' Her frown deepened. 'Okay, so the thing is... Logically, the murder charge would do the business, wouldn't it?'

'What do you mean?'

'Well. If Taylor had enough evidence, which it sounds like they do, Irvine would go away to prison for the murder in Glasgow. End of story.'

'He'd deny it. Tell everyone he was innocent.'

'Okay, but nobody would believe him. He's been in custody for it, that's enough for us to take it incredibly seriously. I haven't seen it in a while, but I think the forensics were pretty tight. Someone killed John McStay and there was enough evidence that it was Sammy Irvine.' She was smiling now. 'What evidence have you got that he's innocent?'

'Not much. Just the word of a murderer via his grandfather.'

'Jesus, Rakesh. You can't just blunder in accusing him without proof of Sammy's innocence.'

'I know that. Look, the reason I believe there might be something in it is... Eric said Sammy thought his location had been leaked. And he thought that was by Taylor.'

'As in, he knew he was at that caravan park?'

'Right.'

'Why? Why is that a thing?'

'Well. Someone must've sent Templeton there to kill Sammy.'

'Right.' She nodded at her computer. 'I think I might've just found you something to help.'

'What?'

Her forehead creased. 'I think you could be onto something. Let me see.' She snapped on a pair of blue gloves and opened the evidence bag on the table. Contained a black lump of plastic, more like charcoal than anything. It might be a phone. 'This is the Nokia I found at the caravan. It's so old it probably can't do 2G let alone 5.' Took a bit of scraping but she got the back off. Sure enough, it was a mobile phone. A bit of off-white battery fell out. 'And the internals are actually okay, especially the SIM card.' She eased it out and snapped it into a reader hanging out of the side of her machine. 'There we go.' She smiled at him. 'Considering you're a newbie, this is good work.'

'You think it's Sammy's phone?'

'Well, I think it's either his, Paul Templeton's or maybe someone else had left it there.'

'So which is it?'

'I don't know. But if you're right and Taylor's a— Well, let's just see.' She went into the phone records system and entered a number, then ran her finger down the screen. 'Aye, just as I thought. Pay-as-you-go SIM. No texts. No calls made, only one received.' She clicked a link. 'Made from... Huh.' She drilled her thumbs off the table. 'You've got something here.'

'Sorry, but I don't follow?'

'Not that I've been in any of the interviews, but Andrea Elliot was saying that they were going on the assumption it was a drunken fight that got out of hand. All throughout, Sammy insisted someone had sent Templeton to kill him. Forced his way in, then came at him. She asked me to get evidence of it, which I haven't found.' She tapped the laptop's edge. 'Until now. A one-time burner like this is a classic sign of a hit. I've dealt with a few of them over the years in Edinburgh. You memorise a number, then call it if you want the hit to happen.' She clicked a link. 'We don't know who owns the phone, that's why it's called a burner phone. You use it once, you toss it. End of story. But whoever received that call went to Gillespie's caravan park.'

'Where was it received?'

'Edinburgh. Princes Street.'

'Okay. A week ago last Friday.'

'Two days before Templeton was killed.' Rakesh thought it through. 'If it was Templeton's burner... And Irvine definitely wasn't in Edinburgh then... It looks like someone tipped him off. Which gave him two days to monitor Irvine's movements. Right?'

'Right. Exactly. Obviously, it didn't go down like he'd planned. Somehow Sammy turned the tables on him.'

Rakesh was starting to see it. He had a tingling deep in his gut, soon replaced by a sick bitterness in his mouth. 'Okay, I can see your logic but we're still missing the why. Why would Taylor frame Irvine for a murder? It flushed him out of Glasgow, sent him down to the Borders, where he's hidden out for a few weeks. Then we jump to a phone call and Templeton trying and failing to kill him. How did they know Irvine was down here?'

'Well, that's not my puzzle to solve, I'm afraid.'

'No, it's mine.' Rakesh stared up at the ceiling, which seemed to be sagging under the weight of something heavy on the floor above. 'What about the other phone?'

'Other phone?'

'Someone called Templeton's burner. Right?'

'Let me see.' Back to the input screen, then the computer started thinking about it for a bit too long. Then it beeped. 'Okay, so the other phone was in Galashiels.'

'An old mobile like that, it's going to be a huge area. Right?'

'Who said anything about an old mobile?' She brought up a map, unfamiliar to Rakesh, of a long, thin town split by a river. 'It was made from a payphone outside the station.'

Rakesh recognised the streets now – that was where he'd pulled in to let Jolene out. Where Sammy had been. He couldn't remember seeing a phone box, but there was one there. He looked around the place, then shut his eyes. 'Crap.'

'You're starting to believe that call was made by Taylor, aren't you?'

'Starting to.' Rakesh leaned back and listened to her fingers clattering across the keyboard. 'Wait. This call was last week. Well, Friday the week before last. Taylor was in Glasgow.'

'Nope.'

'What?'

'He was right here.'

Rakesh jerked forward. 'What?'

She had the station's entry logs up on her screen. 'Swiped in here at the back of ten last Friday. Left at two. That call was made five minutes later.'

What did that show?

Evidence of something. But what?

Someone had tipped off Templeton, arranged for him to kill Sammy Irvine.

Callum Taylor had been here.

Crap.

Rakesh ran his hand down his face but the truth was still there, clinging on to him. 'Whoever made that call knew Irvine was at the caravan park, right?'

'Must've done.'

'What was Taylor up to here?'

'Now that I don't know. You'd need to ask him.'

Aye, and Rakesh didn't know who he could trust. There was enough smoke here to hand this over to the professionals.

CHAPTER FIFTEEN

Rakesh walked through the open-plan area towards the printer. Thankfully it had actually printed. And nobody had swiped his print. The page was still warm, with that fresh-rain smell.

He folded the sheet, scanning the office. A fair few officers still lingering around, not out in the community going door-to-door to find Sammy Irvine.

Didn't seem like anyone had anything anywhere near a result.

Elliot's door was open. Her voice boomed out. 'Jim! Listen to me!'

Rakesh sucked in a deep breath, tried to ignore the screaming inside his head as he strolled over. He passed a desk and stopped.

Jolene was working at her computer, head down, hammering away at the keyboard. She spotted him and stopped typing. Hit the boss key and switched windows to a spreadsheet. 'Hey, Shunty.' She was blushing.

He didn't know what she'd been up to there. Probably sending Elliot a snide email about him. But he didn't really care. He tried to let things bounce off him. Tried to. 'Have you finished with Eric Mitchell?'

'Kind of.'

'Kind of?'

'Well, he's having a word with his lawyer.'

'Great. Still nothing on Irvine?'

'Nope.' She flipped back to her email. A holiday request.

Rakesh was getting really paranoid. 'Thanks for the update.' He walked over to Elliot's office.

Empty.

What the hell? She'd just been in there?

Smelled of stale cigarettes, but a coffee mug smoked away on the desk so she must be nearby.

Rakesh turned heel and came face to face with Jolene. 'Oh, hey.'

'She went to take a call.'

Lot of that going on around here.

The cops here all came from multiple MITs but,

rather than band together, they seemed to want to report back to their own bosses first.

'Have you seen DS Taylor?'

'Not for a wee while.' Jolene was looking at the sheet of paper in his hand, so he folded it in half again and pocketed it. 'Why?'

'Just want to speak to him, that's all. When did you last hear from him?'

'Eh, he called me about half an hour ago.'

'Okay. Well, if he gets in touch again, tell him I'm looking for him.'

'Will do.'

Elliot barged between them, reeking of smoke. 'Out of the way, love birds.'

Rakesh followed her into the office. 'Ma'am, I need a word.'

Elliot scowled at him, then looked at Jolene. 'Are you two ganging up on me?'

'No.'

Jolene scowled at Rakesh. 'No way.'

Rakesh looked at Jolene, but couldn't figure out why she'd said 'no way'. 'Constable, I need a word with DI Elliot in private.'

'Oh, okay.'

'Thanks.' Rakesh kicked the door shut and focused on Elliot.

She slumped behind her desk and slurped at her coffee, grimacing at the taste. 'This just gets better, Shunty. Glasgow are sending two cars full of detectives to help with the search for Irvine.'

'Sounds good.' Rakesh took the seat in front of her desk. 'Have you seen DS Taylor?'

'He's leading the hunt for Sammy Irvine.' She scowled at the taste of her coffee. 'Got every single uniformed constable out with him.' She thunked her mug back down. 'Sammy Irvine was on Channel Street. Round the sodding corner from here.'

'Have you spoken to him?'

She narrowed her eyes at him. 'Why are you asking?'

'No real reason.'

Elliot walked over. 'What's going on here?'

Put up or shut up time.

Rakesh walked over to her, heart hammering in his chest. He had this. He had it. 'I think we might have an issue.' He took out the sheet of paper from his pocket and handed it to her. 'Read that.'

Elliot raised her eyebrows and chuckled, but didn't say anything. She walked over to the desk, grabbed her cup and drank coffee as she read. 'Paul Templeton. Remind me?'

'This is your case.'

'Aye, Sergeant, but I want *your* take on it.'

Fine...

'Templeton's the charred corpse in Sammy Irvine's caravan. Involved in a post office robbery in Troon three weeks ago. Injured the postmaster by hitting him with a baseball bat. Fractured his skull. We don't know where he was hiding out before his body was found at Castle Gillespie holiday park. DS Taylor had a random tip off, found Templeton dead, presumably killed by Sammy Irvine, who was himself badly injured. Gas was leaking from the cooker and the subsequent explosion wiped the whole place clean. We lost evidence that would secure Irvine's conviction for the murder of Templeton. We can still prosecute him, but not for that murder.'

'Right, full marks. What's your point, caller?'

'First, there's a gap between him leaving Troon and DS Taylor finding his body at the caravan park. Second, it looks to me like the murder of Templeton could just as easily have been self-defence.' Rakesh gave her another sheet of paper. 'We found a burner phone at the caravan. Charred, but it was intact enough for Kirsten to get a number from the SIM. She ran it and found that it only received one call. The call came from a phone box outside this station.'

Elliot was frowning. 'What?'

'Just outside, yes. Around the corner on Channel Street.'

'What are you saying?'

'From Irvine's statement, Templeton barged into his caravan, asked Irvine a few questions, then attacked him.'

'Okay.'

'I think someone leaked his location to Templeton.'

'Wait. You think Sammy Irvine's *innocent?*'

'It's possible. Ma'am, I'm thinking someone leaked Sammy Irvine's location to Paul Templeton so he could kill him.'

She slammed her cup back on the desk. 'I don't get it.'

'Ma'am, DS Callum Taylor was an investigating officer on both the post office robbery and Irvine's murder of John McStay.'

'What?'

'I checked. He's connected to—'

'You're saying *Taylor* leaked this?'

'I'm saying it's possible. Sammy told his grandfather he was being framed by Taylor. And there's a lot of evidence stacking up for me here.'

'Jesus Christ.' Elliot buried her head in her hands, massaging her scalp. She sat up, got out her phone and called someone. Then shook her head. 'DS Taylor, it's DI Elliot. Call me.'

'I've tried calling him too, ma'am, but there was no answer.'

Elliot got up and walked over to the door. She popped her head out. 'Jolene, can you get DS Taylor in here, please?'

'On it, ma'am.'

Elliot slammed the door behind her, then walked over to the whiteboard. She uncapped the pen with a loud sucking noise. Then recapped it and turned to face him. 'What's your game here, Shunty?'

'There's no game here.'

'Okay. Why are you doing this, then?'

'You've said it yourself, this case is a disaster. You've been brought down here to fix this. I'm helping you make sure we're doing the right thing.'

'Why, thank you.' Elliot tossed the pen back onto the lip under the whiteboard. 'What are you actually saying?'

'One of us is calling Professional Standards and Ethics.'

'You're threatening me? Seriously?'

'I'm not—'

The door opened and Taylor strolled in, hands in

pockets. 'Woah, Andi, look like you're going to kill him. I can come back?'

She snorted. 'Shut the door behind you.'

Taylor frowned. 'O-kay...' He complied then sat. 'Looks like a funeral and not a particularly funny one.'

'No.' Elliot shook her head. 'Oh, it's a funeral for Shunty here.'

Taylor laughed. 'Why, what's he done?'

Rakesh needed to take charge of this. 'I found, em, that... Eh.'

'Come on, Shunty. Accuse DS Taylor to his face, why don't you?'

'Eh, well... Eh?'

Taylor folded his arms. 'Accuse me of what?'

Rakesh coughed into his fist. 'You investigated both of their crimes, right?'

Taylor smirked. 'You need to be a bit clearer in your questioning, son.'

'You worked both the post office robbery Paul Templeton was involved in and also the murder of John McStay.'

'McStay? Sure, I worked it. That's how MITs operate, as I'm sure you'll find out soon enough when you actually get round to doing the job you've been hired for.'

Rakesh passed him the sheets of paper, his hand

shaking.

'What's this?' Taylor laughed again as he read it. 'Somebody made a phone call?'

'That call was made by someone near here to Paul Templeton two days before he tried to murder Sammy Irvine. It's evidence that someone's leaked the location, allowing Templeton to—'

Taylor laughed. 'You think *I* did it?'

'Well. You were here at that time.'

'No, I wasn't.'

'You were.' Rakesh produced the security system print from Kisten and handed it over. 'There it is in black and white. You were *here*. Not in Glasgow. Did you—'

'Okay...' Taylor checked the pages and ran his tongue across his lips. 'I'm pretty hungry, so I could do with getting my lunch.' He put the pages down. 'Can I get you anything, Andi?'

Rakesh got up and walked over to the door, blocking them getting out, or anyone else getting in. 'You're not leaving until you tell us the truth.'

'This is complete bollocks.' Taylor walked over to the whiteboard, smirking away. 'Andi, what's going on here?' He snarled at Rakesh like a rat backed into a corner, then sat down in a flourish of splayed jacket. Something thudded off the seat back. 'Go on, then.'

'We've got proof you weren't in Glasgow when the call was made. You were here, in this station. Ask me, that's a weird coincidence.'

'That's bollocks. Absolute bollocks!'

'It's not.' Rakesh waved the sheet at him. 'Why were you here?'

Taylor stared up at the ceiling. The machinery whirred away behind his eyes, cogs and gears. Conjuring up new lies. Some fresh explanation for his chicanery. He scratched at his neck, then looked at Elliot, his eyes like a small kid caught stealing biscuits. 'Come on...'

She smoothed her fringe over with her fingers. Took two goes. 'Take your time, Taylor. It's all fine.'

'I... Okay, let me check my notebook.' Taylor got it out and flicked through the pages. 'Huh. I was here.' He checked the sheet. 'Sorry, I forgot. Been under a lot of stress recently.' He laughed, quick and without humour. 'Lot of pressure to find Sammy Irvine, sure you can imagine.' He stared at Rakesh. 'Happy now?'

'Not really.' Elliot folded her arms. 'Why were you here?'

'I haven't done anything.'

'A man is being accused of murder and you're not giving us straight answers. Why were you here?'

'What do you think's going on here?'

'You're not giving me any evidence back. You're just trying to deny it. Makes me think he might actually be being framed.'

His laugh was full of humour. 'Shunty, Sammy Irvine's as guilty as a puppy in a puddle. Listen. You didn't see what he did to John McStay. His head was... I'll never...' Taylor stared into space. He got to his feet and started pacing around the interview room, shaking his head. Pleading with Elliot, arms out wide. 'Come on, Andi, this is absolute nonsense!'

Rakesh stood up, getting as close to eye level as he could manage. 'Here's what I think happened. You caught the murder case. But Sammy was in the wind. You were getting your arse kicked over it. Then, somehow, you found out where Sammy Irvine was. But you didn't go and arrest him, did you? Maybe your prosecution wasn't looking too promising. Sammy Irvine either seemed innocent or the evidence didn't stack up to a solid conviction. But you were getting pressured. You needed closure to it. So you called Paul Templeton, told him where Irvine was. Templeton's a violent man. Does things for money. You expected him to kill Irvine. It'd solve two huge problems for you.'

Taylor grinned at Rakesh. 'That right, aye?'

'Tell me what's wrong with it.'

'Oh. Shit. There's nothing wrong with it.' Taylor

held out his hands. 'You've caught me, fair and square. And I would've got away with it if it wasn't for your twenty minutes of policing experience.'

Rakesh felt that bead of sweat trickle down his forehead. 'Eh?'

'You daft bastard. Do you honestly think I did this?'

'It seems to fit.'

'Seems to. Right. Great. Let's arrest anyone it "seems to" fit. Bloody hell, Andi, where did you get this clown from? Is this some kind of fly-on-the-wall thing?' He looked around the room. 'Is Jeremy Beadle going to jump out, dressed as a policeman?'

'No. He's dead.' Elliot picked up her coffee. 'So, did you do it?'

'Nope. No, ma'am, I did not. Uh-uh.'

'Cool.' Elliot finally took a sip, grimaced and put it back down. 'Well, that's that settled then. No more nonsense from you, Shunty. Okay?'

Rakesh felt his gut fall through the floor. 'What?'

'Thinking I might go to Markies and get some pork pies and scotch eggs for the team.' Elliot took another drink of coffee. 'There's always some *vegan* who wants sushi, though.'

'You can't be serious?'

Elliot rolled her eyes at him. 'Are you the vegan, Shunty?'

'No, but—'

'So you'll have a pork pie?'

'I don't eat pork.'

She looked over at Taylor. 'See what I mean?'

Rakesh pointed at him. 'He's lying to your face!'

'No, Shunty. He's a cop with twenty years' experience instead of twenty minutes.'

Taylor was nodding. 'Listen, pal. If I'd known where Irvine was, he'd be in cuffs and behind bars. You're the one who let him go.'

'But you had a lead—'

'I had a lead on *Templeton's* location. I took some cops out to that manky caravan park. That's why we found them both. One of my bloody team died there.'

Milking it…

'This was after Templeton attacked Irvine. You expected to find his body, didn't you?'

'I had nothing to do with this!' Taylor clenched his fists, staring right at Rakesh. Shaking. Teeth bared. Nostrils flaring. Looked like he was going to lash out and punch him. 'Problem you've got, Shunty, is you've got no facts, just wild theories.'

'What were you doing here a week ago on Friday?'

'I was interviewing Victor Carter. A known associate of Paul Templeton. Word was he knew where he was. He didn't. But he knew someone who knew someone. Two days later and we found someone who had seen Templeton, heard he was going to Castle Gillespie.'

Crap.

Elliot snorted. Eyes shut. Rubbing her temples. 'DS Siyal, can you give us a moment, please?'

Rakesh swallowed. 'Aren't you going to—'

'What did you think would happen? A confetti cannon going off? Dancing girls? The Chief Constable coming here to promote you to superintendent on day one? You've over-reached here, you bloody idiot.'

'You're not taking my concerns seri—'

'I've listened. I've let you raise them with DI Taylor. To his face. But this isn't good for you, son. I warned you about stepping out of line on your first day. Aside from letting a murder suspect escape, this is so far over the line, you've no idea where the line is.'

'You're mixing your meta—'

'Enough!' She pointed at the door. 'Leave. Now!'

Rakesh smiled at her. Left the room with a shaking feeling running up and down his legs.

Outside, the office noise swelled around him. Almost knocked him over.

He was the one who was getting hauled over the coals for this…

Aye.

Because he'd really messed up.

'You okay there?' Kirsten was standing to the side, head tilted towards him.

'I need my lunch.'

'That's it? You're in there for ages and you need your lunch?'

Rakesh didn't have the words to reply. His first day on the job and he'd cocked it all up. So much for making a difference to society – he'd made a complete mess of his career.

First day and he'd really dropped a bollock.

Talk about a false start.

'Shunty, what's up?'

'Well. I accused Taylor and... They didn't take it seriously.'

'That's outrageous.'

'Well. I don't think it was him who leaked. Him and Elliot are discussing how to sack me. Probably got some probationary clause in my contract and...' He wanted to cry. Felt the tears welling up. In front of a whole audience of people ready and raring to watch the new guy crumple.

The office door opened and Elliot stormed out, swooshing her jacket around her shoulders. 'Come on, Shunty. You and me have an appointment in Edinburgh.'

CHAPTER SIXTEEN

Elliot was driving them into Edinburgh. Wouldn't speak but they were clearly heading for Fettes, the old Lothian and Borders headquarters, now just an office they were actively trying to sell off to property developers.

Where Human Resources was located.

They were going to sack him.

Already.

Day one, hoofed off the job.

Well done, Shunty.

He ignored his aching gut and tried to centre himself by focusing on the streets.

Lights were on already at just after two.

The whole city was shrouded in steady drizzle, which could turn to black ice later. Still, Edinburgh had thawed and this morning's threat of snow had dissolved with it. Thing about taking the bus was he didn't have to head back south to get his car. Just another bus across town.

They passed the Commonwealth Pool, where Rakesh swam twice a week, every week. His own flat was opposite, his home for the last few years. His brother had it at university, and he'd taken it over. Two years training, then six working as a full-time lawyer. Then his stint over at Tulliallan, training to be a cop.

What the hell was he going to do now?

'I'm sorry.'

She looked over at him. 'Sorry?'

'For accusing DI Taylor.'

'Right. Well, sorry's not really going to cut it.' She was baring her teeth. 'Son, you're so green you squeak when you walk. I have bras older than you.'

'You're only ten years older than me.'

'Feels like I'm dealing with a child, though. You're useless, Shunty. A liability. You don't know *anything*.'

Instead of heading straight on for the centre, Elliot pulled into the lane past St Leonards police station.

What the hell?

She trundled into the car park at the back and took a space just by the entrance. She killed the engine and got out first. 'Come on, then.'

'I thought we were going to Fettes?'

She frowned at him, her fringe hanging over her eyes. 'Fettes? Why?'

'So you can take me to HR.'

'HR? Why would I do that?'

'For accusing DS Taylor of—'

Elliot laughed. 'Listen, I tried. Called up my contact there, but they wouldn't have it. Not on your first day. I mean, I get it. It's not for you. You're hopeless. In my mind, you should be let go. Let you find something you can do. Counting paperclips. Driving a bus. Doing a second degree. Who knows. Must be something.'

'So where are we—'

'I spoke to Pringle and he said I should just coach you better, counsel you on jumping to conclusions. Then if it becomes a trend, file an incident report on you. Get you on an actioned contract.'

Rakesh was sweating in the cold. 'So why are we here?'

'Because I'm going to try to unload you to another team instead.'

'Come on. DS Taylor doesn't exactly seem innocent over this.'

'Shunty, Shunty, Shunty. I appreciate people speaking up, really I do. A lot of cops wouldn't. It takes guts to stand up and be counted. But you were totally wrong. You had the square root of hee haw in terms of evidence, just the word of the suspect's grandfather.'

'I had—'

'—some bits of paper. That's it. Nothing substantive in the slightest.' She sighed. 'You honestly thought you had something, didn't you?'

'I still think it.'

'I'm not celebrating your gumption here, Shunty, I'm tearing you a new arsehole. But I've got your number now. And I'll make sure Scott and Ally know all about you.'

Rakesh didn't know what to say to that.

She got out and set off across the car park.

Rakesh followed her, but he just wanted to grab his backpack off the seat and go home. Get in the bath and forget all about this. This massive mistake. Huge. He was able to walk across the tarmac without any fear.

Elliot held the door for him. 'You take your time. I mean, the last thing you want to do is slip on your arse.' She let go and entered.

She knew.

Of course she knew.

Jolene and her were thick as thieves.

He got there and followed her inside.

Elliot waved to the desk sergeant as she swiped them through. The corridor was dark, like the overhead lights hadn't triggered or nobody had bothered to switch them on. Or nobody cared it was this dark.

A man paced towards them, hands in pockets. Immaculate suit, short hair, soul patch lurking under his bottom lip. 'Hey, Andi.'

She stopped to smile at him. 'Scott.'

He was frowning. 'Thought you were down in the Borders?'

'Aye, but it's not exactly that far away, is it? I'll send you a postcard from sunny Melrose if you're a good boy.'

'You live down there, don't you?'

'Aye, Gala is ten minutes down the road. And those roads are always gritted, no matter how brutal the weather.'

'Hell of a drive up here in winter.'

'Telling me, Scott, especially coming over the Lammermuirs. You know you're in trouble when they've got those snow depth poles at the side of the road.'

He laughed. 'Been a while since I went down that way.'

She fixed Scott with a hard look. 'Actually, you got a minute, Sundance?'

He winced. 'Not heard that in a wee while, Ballbuster.' He opened the door to a meeting room and stepped in.

Rakesh made to follow.

Elliot pressed her hand against his chest. 'Wait here.' She gave a flash of her eyebrows and followed Scott into the room.

Leaving him standing there like a child.

Great.

Took thirty seconds for the first raised voice, him saying, 'No.'

'Come on, Scott.'

'I don't have any space on my team. I've got one too many sergeants as it is.'

'What about you being two DCs short?'

Rakesh didn't want to listen to it. Being bargained away like that, horse-traded. He walked off down the corridor until he couldn't hear the words, just the din resonating through the door.

Crap.

He'd let a suspect go.

Totalled a car.

Accused a colleague of organising a hit.

What the hell was he thinking?

Absolute bloody idiot.

The door slammed and Elliott stomped towards him with a face like frozen sick. 'Well, he isn't in the mood for any more liability, so I've got to keep you for now, Shunty.'

'So we've driven all this way just to—'

'Oh, there are plenty of other people I can call in favours with. Someone has to be short-staffed. Surely there's a village that's short of its idiot.' She smiled at him. 'But for now, you're my idiot.' She trotted off down the corridor and stopped outside the only door not marked with a number, stuck between two and four.

Most places, you could guess it was a three, but in a police station? Never assume – as a lawyer, Rakesh had ended up in cupboards more than once when searching for his clients. Dirty tricks played on lawyers and those they represented.

Elliot put her hand on the door.

'You going to tell me why we're here?'

'Killing two birds with one stone.' She looked around at him. 'After you let Irvine get away, DS Taylor took charge of the hunt and focused on tracking down Vic Carter.'

'Who's he?' Rakesh frowned. 'Wait. Gillespie told us he'd been drinking with Irvine at the caravan park?'

'Correct.' Elliott folded her arms. 'He's how he found Paul Templeton's location. Here are the ground rules, Shunty. Say nothing, touch nothing, think nothing.

You're window dressing. If you do that, then perhaps I might let you prove that you're capable of fetching tea from time to time.' She opened the door and entered.

Inside, Vic Carter sat like he was expecting his main course to be served, bemused it was taking so long to arrive. Mid-forties but his hair was all white – a silver fox, cleanshaven and cherubic. His body odour wasn't fully masked by the room's reek of bleach – a mix of sweat and stale booze. 'Finally.' His voice was dark and smoky like an Islay whisky. 'Thought I'd maybe done something I shouldn't have.' He laughed, eyes rapidly scanning them as they sat.

Aside from the role-play training sessions at Tulliallan – and his embarrassing five minutes with Sammy Irvine that morning, which he was surprised hadn't become another nickname – Rakesh had never been on this side of an interview room table before. He was used to sitting to the suspect's left or right. Noting everything down, interjecting and advising his client by the time-honoured tradition of a whisper in the ear. Acting like a total dickhead because he had to – his clients were marginalised and innocent, or swore they were, and needed his help to avoid miscarriages of justice.

All until that wasn't enough and he could see how

much the deck was stacked against people like him. People like Sammy Irvine.

Samir Erdoğan.

Assuming that was all true.

Now, sat directly opposite Vic Carter, Rakesh was unsure where to look. What to do. How to act. He took a deep breath, but it didn't make his throat feel any clearer.

Elliot knew precisely what to do. She shrugged off her coat, slapped her notebook in front of her and flashed a smile. 'Victor, right?'

'Vic, please.'

She thrust out a hand. 'DI Andrea Elliot. This is DS Siyal.'

'So.' Vic shifted in his seat, uncomfortable. The faintest whiff of second-hand booze, like it was sifting out through his pores. 'How can I help you guys?'

'Gather you work as a chef down in Galashiels?'

'That's right.'

'The big hotel up near the hospital.'

'What of it?'

'Bit out of your way, isn't it? Leith lad like you?'

'The Borders railway is great. Into Edinburgh in less than an hour.'

'It is great, I'll give you that.' She nodded slowly. 'Talk to me about November.'

'November?'

'Gather you were staying at Castle Gillespie.'

'Ah, right.'

'Sounds like there's a tale there?'

'It's a long one. And I don't have much time to spill it.'

'Well, DS Siyal and me don't have anywhere else to be.'

'Right.' Vic scratched at the hair on the back of his head. 'Okay, so I lost my job on bonfire night. Working in a new place just off Broughton Street. Pinko's Gin Palace, it's called. I...' He chuckled. 'Accidentally set off a box of sparklers in the store room. Lost three thousand burgers.'

'Three *thousand*?'

'Aye. Shouldn't have been in the same room as the fireworks, should it, but it's done now.'

'So how did you end up staying at Castle Gillespie?'

'Well. Because of that wee incident, I split up with my ex, eh?'

'Don't see how that follows?'

'Well, she doesn't like me smoking, but I have a fag after a shag. It wasn't so much the burgers I got sacked for as smoking in the store room. It was perishing outside, no way I'm heading out there for a fag.' Vic frowned. 'Got into trouble from the owner for calling a cigarette that. Can't say anything these days, can you?'

A smile flashed over Elliot's lips. 'So you lost your job?'

'Aye. Couldn't find a new one. So she kicked me out. Think she's been seeing someone else, like, but... Well. She didn't want anything to do with me. So I needed a place to crash while I figured my shite out. Me and Fred Gillespie go back a long time, so he gave a cheap rate for a van that wasn't in the best of nick, but beggars can't be choosers. Stopped off at the Eskbank Tesco on the way down, filled the motor full of booze, Corn Flakes and Pot Noodles. Long-life milk. Carling. Twenty fags a day for two months. Great internet down at the Castle, so I just needed my wee Fire stick. Thought I'd lie low at the caravan park for a bit until my ship came in.'

'That ship was your job?'

'Aye, aye.'

'You speak to anyone while you were there?'

'Few lads, aye. Most didn't look you in the eye, so I got the message. Few good laughs, though, you know. Freezing outside at that time of year, but one of them got a fire pit going outside his. Not too cold when you're wearing a voddie jacket.' He cackled. 'Played a few hands of poker.'

'Sounds like fun.'

Vic shrugged his shoulders. 'Had worse Novembers, like.'

'Any names?'

Vic narrowed his eyes now. 'What's this about?'

'Just wondering if you could help us with an inquiry. Would mean a lot to me, personally.'

'Eh, well. There was Fud. Mango Pete. And Wee Sammy.'

Elliot jotted them down, not giving any reaction. 'When did you move out?'

'Well, kind of a grey area.'

'Grey how?'

Vic reached out his arms and started singing, 'I saw my ship come sailing in on Christmas Eve in the morning.' He sat back, looking bemused at the lack of reaction. 'Found a job in Gala, covering Christmas and New Year. Never been so busy, but it was grand. Boy kept me on after. I'd been driving there and back, but the commute was a bugger at that time of year. Got pulled over once in the morning. A bawhair under the limit, so I took that as a warning. Owner had a flat down in the town, needed a tenant. Job's a good 'un! So I left Chateau Gillespie and been staying in Gala ever since. Trying to keep my head down.'

Elliot was nodding along with the convoluted tale.

'And yet my colleagues picked you up from an address in Gracemount in the wee hours of this morning?'

'Right.' Vic snorted and looked away. 'Got myself into a wee bit of bother, eh?'

'Want to tell us about it?'

Vic sat there, rubbing his hands together, then gave a 'sod it' shrug. 'Went back to see my kid's mother. Had this daft idea I could buy a flat down in Gala and we could all live together. Three of us, eh? And everything would be okay.'

'But?'

'But she wasn't happy seeing me.'

'You were drunk, weren't you?'

'Had a bit in me, aye.'

'A bit? I can still smell it from here.'

'Listen.' Vic collapsed back in his chair and slowly ran his hand down his face. 'Whatever you want out of me, you can forget it.'

'Come on, Vic. Just—'

'Seriously.' He sat back, arms folded. 'Whatever this is about, I'm not helping you. If you're going to treat me with disrespect like that, you can ram it.'

He'd given them so much, but this Wee Sammy he'd mentioned…

That had to be him. Right?

Elliot waited for eye contact before smiling. 'Vic.

From what I gather, you were picked up after your ex-partner called the police. But that's not what we're asking you about. We're not here to prosecute you for that, okay?'

'What *do* you want to know, then?'

'Last Friday, you were in the Galashiels police station, right?'

'And?'

'Who were you speaking to?'

'Some weegie cop. Can't remember his name. Big twat. Tall. Asking me all these questions about Sammy Irvine.'

'You know Sammy, right?'

'Do I?'

'You mentioned a Wee Sammy to him.'

'Oh. Right, him. Aye. Used to drink with the boy when I was staying at Castle Gillespie. One of the lads around the fire, you know? Boy loved his Polish voddie.' Vic frowned. 'Don't think he was Polish, like.'

'After you met my colleague, DS Callum Taylor, at the Galashiels station, someone made a phone call to Paul Templeton.'

Vic sat there, licking his lips. Said nothing.

'Was that you, Vic?'

'Shite.' Vic shut his eyes. 'So that's what this is all about?'

'You're not denying it.'

'Not saying it was me, either.'

'How did you know Templeton?'

'Worked together in the kitchens at the Debonair off Lothian Road.'

'I know the place. A whole murky world there, involving drugs.' Elliot raised a finger. 'But that's not our game here, either. I just care about the phone number Templeton gave you.'

'Nope.'

Elliot laughed. 'Nope?'

'Saying nowt.'

'You called Paul Templeton, didn't you?' Elliot held his gaze.

Vic sat back. 'Nope.'

'You daft sod. You might've thought you were smart by using a phone box to call a burner number, but there's CCTV there. Clocked you going into the phone box at the time the call was made. Only person in it an hour each way.'

'Shite.'

Rakesh sat back, frowning.

Crap.

She knew.

Elliot knew.

When he was spilling his guts about his theory,

about how Taylor had been the one to pass it on, Elliot had known it was bollocks. Known it was Vic Carter who made the call…

He'd snared himself in a trap.

She was right – what an absolute clown he was.

Vic was drumming his fingers on the table. 'Sod it. Aye. Paul said if I ever needed to speak to him, call this number. Advised not using it unless it was a dire emergency. And I was in a police interview room like this but down in Gala. Taylor was asking me all these questions. He thought I knew where Sammy was, but the truth was I just didn't tell him.'

Elliot shook her head. 'And instead of telling DS Taylor, you called Paul Templeton as soon as you got out of the station, right? Gave him Sammy's location. Right?'

Vic shifted his gaze between them, then stared into the distance. He swallowed hard. 'I called him, aye.'

'You hear what happened afterwards?'

'No, and I don't care.' Vic held up his hands. 'Hard to feel guilty about anything when you're as skint as I am. Put the money in my kid's savings account.'

'Templeton *paid* you?'

'Bollocks.' Vic shut his eyes. 'A grand, aye.'

'For some information on where to find Sammy Irvine?'

'Aye. My motto is "don't ask, don't tell". And also, look after your own.'

'How did you know?'

'Bumped into the boy in Edinburgh, didn't I? In seeing my kid, there's big Paul hiding out down a back street.'

'You know where Sammy Irvine is now?'

Vic looked away. 'Nope.'

'That the truth?'

'Aye. God's honest truth.'

Elliot clattered her elbows off the desktop and got Vic's attention. 'Mr Carter, Paul Templeton was injured in a fight with Mr Irvine. We're not one hundred percent sure if he was dead before the fire broke out, but our pathologist believes he was.'

'*Fire?*'

'Mr Templeton's remains were found in Sammy Irvine's caravan after it burnt down. It appears he was killed while attacking Mr Irvine.'

Vic's pink face was now a shade of grey as light as his hair. 'Ah, shite.'

'So you can see why you continuing to help us will be looked upon very favourably.'

'But I haven't done anything!'

'Sure. Vic. We're just here to ask you these questions

about the death of Paul Templeton. Now, one last time – do you know where Sammy Irvine is?'

'Okay, here's the deal. I do know where he is, but I'm not telling you any more until I know for sure I'm getting out of here without a charge. Scot free. Okay?'

'So much for the God's honest truth...' Elliot nodded. 'We can't arrange that. Just tell us where he is.'

'Deal or I'm staying quiet.'

'There's no deal on the table, obviously, but if you help us find Sammy Irvine, we can put in a good word for you with the arresting officers.'

'A good word? Come on, you think I was born last week? You honestly think my ex is going to drop those charges?'

'I'm not talking about the domestic. I'm talking about you drink driving your way there to shout dog's abuse at her.'

'Fuck.'

'Vic, the way I see it, you could get let off with a warning for that. But someone with your record... Coupled with the domestic... You could also go back inside for what you did.'

Vic started shaking his head. 'Can't do any more time. Seriously.'

'Okay, but if you tell us where he is, we can—'

'Fine. Deal.' Vic's hungry eyes shifted between them. 'Keep me out of jail and I'm all yours.'

'That's not the deal, Vic. You help us find him, we'll see what we can do.'

'Okay. So Sammy called me. Said he needed a place to crash. I had a place. Well. Knew of one, anyway.'

'In Galashiels?'

He nodded.

'Where?'

'There's a brass Yale on my keyring, which is with all my stuff. You put in that word, sweetheart, then get yourself down to Gala and I'll tell you where it is when you get there, assuming it's all looking rosy for me.'

'That's not going to happen.'

'Okay.'

Elliot got to her feet. 'We'll head back to Galashiels without putting that word in. Wave goodbye to that license. Or seeing your kid.'

'Oh, come on! I've given you bucketloads here!'

'Hardly. Soon as it gets interesting, you clam up. Now. You tell us where he is, we find him, then I'll put in that word.'

CHAPTER SEVENTEEN

Elliot pulled into the Galashiels police station car park. Three squad cars sat there, engines idling. She parked in one of the spaces furthest away and got out, then charged over to the smoking shelter.

Rakesh got out into the cold and followed her over, breathing in Elliot's second-hand smoke. He stopped upwind of her but was standing in Taylor's cloud of mint-flavoured vape.

Taylor was eyeing him suspiciously, but didn't look like he was going to lamp Rakesh. He took another toot on his vape stick. 'Anything?'

'Nope.' Elliot took a big drag then let it out of her nostrils. 'Still waiting.'

Rakesh checked his watch again. Over an hour since

the interview and the chat with the arresting officers. Enough time to travel from south Edinburgh down to Galashiels, and still nothing from Vic Carter on Sammy's location.

Was he playing them?

Hard to know.

Elliot blew smoke out of the side of her mouth. 'Heard from one of the boys in my old team that her holiness is heading down to the Met in July.'

Taylor laughed. 'Seriously?'

Elliot took another drag. 'DCS, but it'll still be a big pay rise. Course, it'll mean another reshuffle up here.'

'One thing Police Scotland does well is piss about with deckchairs. Orchestra keeps playing.' Taylor sucked on his vape stick. 'Meanwhile the Titanic batters into the iceberg.'

Elliot laughed through a fug of smoke. 'You might get made DI, Taylor.'

'Aye, sure. Not with people accusing me of being bent.' Taylor gave Rakesh some side eye. 'Right?'

Rakesh shrugged.

Elliot raised her eyebrows. 'You're a brave man to joke about it in front of him. Tends to make big assumptions about things. I'm waiting on him to grass to teacher.' Her phone rang and she charged away from them. 'Scott, how's it going?' She pressed her cigarette against the bin and dropped the butt in.

Taylor stared at Rakesh, staring through a cloud of minty vapour. 'Come on, Shunty. It's all fair in love and war.'

'And which is this?'

'Bit of both.'

'Thought you'd be annoyed.'

'Just bemused. I tried to be your pal. But you honestly thought I'd told Templeton? Really?'

'It fit.'

'Sure.'

'But you knew, didn't you? Both of you, you knew that Carter made the call. Let me blunder in there. You just didn't know where Carter was.'

'We were onto him. He was careless. Just didn't know he'd been picked up.'

'I'm sorry for—'

'I hope you learnt a valuable lesson today. Your old gig as a lawyer is all about weaving a narrative about your client being a victim of a corrupt system. Discrediting details to throw away the whole story. Well, when you think like that you miss how important those details are to our side of things. The most important thing is evidence. Not theories. Evidence. And what does the evidence tell you? Where can you get more?

You had a theory based on one statement. A throwaway comment. You found some evidence, sure, but it was based on a flawed theory. If you'd asked anyone, you'd have found the truth.'

'I'm clearly not cut out for—'

'But.' Taylor raised a finger. 'Because of what you and Kirsten did, it underpinned what Andi and I thought. We were searching for evidence we knew was there, but you found it. So well done.'

Rakesh wanted to cry.

After it all, he just wanted to crawl into a ball and sleep.

Elliot charged between them and exhaled her smoke. 'Glad rags on, boys. We are go go go.' She hopped into her car and hared off behind the three squad cars, running blues and twos.

Taylor got into the pool car Rakesh had been given earlier. 'With me, Shunty.'

No other cars, so Rakesh got in the passenger side. Belt on, grabbing hold of the handle above the door.

Taylor spun the wheels as he raced across the thawed car park, then switched the blue lights on and gave a blast of siren. He took a left, driving around the one-way system, past the phone box where Vic Carter had made the fateful call. He hammered through the red light at the end, getting a blared horn from a dark-grey VW four-by-four as he swung right, then up to the roundabout, where he took the left turn behind the convoy of cars. 'You still think Irvine's innocent?'

'Of the murder?'

'No, of bringing down the last government.' Taylor rolled his eyes. 'Yes, the murder.'

'I just want to see what he's got to say for himself. Assuming he's even here.'

Three of the other cars pulled up on Ladhope Brae, just as the road narrowed around parked cars on both sides. Where the bus had driven him that morning. The final squad car parked across the road, blocking the oncoming traffic. Both cops jumped out in their fluorescent jackets, arms windmilling and waving to redirect the traffic back the way. Getting a volley of abuse in return.

Elliot was outside a main door flat. 'Vic Carter's given us approval to enter his address.' She nodded at the bulky uniforms either side of the door. 'Said he's been staying here.'

Rakesh recognised one of them from Eric's flat.

Big Craig.

Elliot tossed him the key. 'In we go.'

Craig opened the door and let himself inside first. 'Police!'

Taylor was next, then Rakesh charged along the

scuffed laminate, heart pounding, gripping his baton like a real cop. He'd swung it so many times in training – hitting a heavy bag was just the same as hitting a person.

Right?

Smelled like something was burning in there.

Sammy Irvine was in the kitchen, hands raised.

'On your knees!' Taylor grabbed his wrist and hauled him down to the floor, then snapped a cuff on his left wrist.

Sammy glanced up at the eye-level grill. 'My cheese on toast is burning!'

Smoke started billowing from the grill.

The alarm blared out.

Taylor looked over at the burning toast.

Sammy punched him in the balls.

Taylor screamed, grabbing his groin.

The flat's other alarms blasted out in a chorus that stung Rakesh's ears.

In the aural maelstrom, Rakesh stepped forward. He moved to swing with his baton, but stopped. Made eye contact with Sammy. It wasn't the same as hitting a bag. Nothing like it. He'd scream, he'd haunt his nightmares.

No.

But he had to do it, so he lashed out.

And missed Sammy by millimetres.

Sammy jerked to the side, his swinging cuff smashing into Taylor's nose.

Another scream, even louder than the alarm.

Sammy grabbed Taylor from behind, pressing a giant knife against his throat. The block on the counter had one missing.

Rakesh hadn't seen him take it. He raised his hands. 'Come on, Sammy. Don't do this.'

'Why not?' Sammy looked at the window, like he wanted to jump out. The original sash and case had long since been replaced by aluminium double-glazing. 'I can get away from you again.'

'It's too much of a drop down to the train tracks here.'

'It's the river, you idiot. I'll be fine.'

'You won't. Might not die, but it'll be a big enough drop to break your neck or back. You'll be paralysed.'

Sammy tightened his grip on the knife, digging the steel into Taylor's throat.

The alarm still blared out, stinging Rakesh's ears.

Taylor gurgled. His eyes were bulging. 'Sammy, let me go.'

'Why? Why should I?' Sammy dug the knife into Taylor's flesh. 'You deserve this!'

Rakesh locked eyes with him and held his gaze. 'Tell

me why you did it, Sammy. Tell me why you're so angry at the police. Why you want to kill a cop.'

Sammy stared at Rakesh with mad eyes. 'I didn't kill him!'

'You did, Sammy. And you're going to kill a cop in front of a room of witnesses.' Rakesh waved around the room. 'You'll go to prison whatever happens. Just don't take Callum here with you.'

'He deserves this! More than anyone! I came to him with all that evidence and he did nothing. You did *nothing*. His inaction killed him.'

'Killed who?'

'Marcin!'

'Sammy, who's Marcin?'

'You don't care!'

And it hit Rakesh – the answer was to the wrong question.

They knew who he'd killed and why he was hiding out in a caravan park down here, dowsing himself in vodka.

It wasn't who did it or how, or even what happened during the murder.

Vic Carter knew Paul Templeton would pay a grand for Sammy's location.

The real question was why?

Why had Sammy killed John McStay in Glasgow?

Why was he hiding out down here?

Why was Templeton after him?

Why was he going to slice Taylor's throat in front of all these cops?

'Sammy. It's not just you who's lost, okay? I'm wondering why I'm here. I'm wondering why I became a cop because, truthfully, I don't seem to be very good at it. I fuck up everything I touch. I don't mean to, but I do. I let you escape. I totalled a car. I accused...' Rakesh kept his distance. Kept his focus on the knife. 'But I look at things differently. I'm not someone who's climbed the career ladder from uniform to being a detective. I used to be a criminal defence lawyer, protecting people like you. Falsely accused. Victims of racism. Maybe that's what you need – someone to ask you a better question so you can explain and people will see you differently. You tell me and I'll listen, my word to you – why did you kill John McStay?'

Sammy pressed the knife tighter around Taylor's throat.

'I want to believe you, Sammy. I want to understand. Let him go and we'll sort this out. Okay? Sammy, you've had to hide out because you can't trust anyone. I get it, I really do. But why did Paul Templeton want to kill you?'

Sammy let the knife slacken off a bit, but still held Taylor.

The flat was now filled with cops. Nobody moved. Just waiting, nobody moving to switch off the alarm.

'Come on, Sammy.' Rakesh raised his hands higher. 'Let him go.'

'But...'

'Killing a police officer like this won't make it any easier for you. Come with me, Sammy. Come and sit with me and talk it all through with me. I want to believe you. Please. Help me to get you off with this.'

Sammy wasn't moving.

'Please. Tell me why you did it. Why did you kill John McStay?'

Sammy looked right at Rakesh, then shut his eyes. He still didn't let Taylor go.

Rakesh cleared his throat. 'Sammy, tell us the truth. The complete truth. If you do that, I can help you. Okay?'

'All I've done since you picked me up last week is tell the truth.'

'All last week, Sammy, you just sat in silence. Didn't answer a single question. That's not the same thing as telling the truth.'

'Hard to be honest when I feel like this.'

'Like what?'

Sammy shrugged. 'You wouldn't understand.'

'Try me.'

'I can't do time!'

'Why?'

'I'm innocent.'

'A lot of people say that, Sammy, but as far as I can tell, you've murdered two men. John McStay and Paul Templeton.'

'Templeton was going to kill me.'

'So you're admitting it?'

'He hit me with a bottle. If I hadn't cut him with some glass, he'd have killed me.'

'If that's the case, why didn't you say it was self-defence?'

'Because it doesn't matter what I said. Does it? You just... You're all the same. You lie. You cheat. You're making me out to be a killer.'

'What makes you think that?'

Sammy looked right at Rakesh, deep into his eyes. 'Because I went to the police and they just laughed in my face.'

'What happened, Sammy?'

'I... They... They didn't...'

'What did you say to them, Sammy?'

'You don't understand.'

'Sammy. Talk to me. Please.'

'Guys like John McStay... He...'

'He what?'

Sammy brushed a hand across his lips. It was shaking. 'John came into my club a few times. Having fun, you know how it is. Acting like the big boy, throwing the money around. Making it rain, like they say. Security caught him doing lines in the toilet. Chucked him out. But... Next thing I know, he's in my office in the daytime. Asking me to pay him three grand a week to make sure nothing bad happens to any of my punters.'

'A protection racket?'

'Right. He was in a gang. I didn't know that. Okay?'

'That why you killed him?'

'No! I paid him! Kept paying it too. My first three grand from every Friday night went to him. Every week. Twenty staff on my payroll plus security. Rates going up, breweries charging more. Things were tight and getting tighter. Some nights I made a hundred quid after all that stress. For a whole week. And John just kept on asking for more money. All the time. Just more money. I was in deep and it was getting deeper.'

'What happened, Sammy?'

'I stopped paying.'

'And?'

'And...' Sammy sighed. A tear was streaming down his cheek. He swallowed hard, shifted his gaze around the room. Didn't seem to notice that he had a knife to a cop's throat. 'John came into the club. And...'

'What happened, Sammy?'

'He...'

'Did you kill him?'

'No.' Sammy brushed a hand across his lips. 'He caught me with... with my boyfriend.'

Rakesh frowned. 'Marcin?'

'Right. Marcin.' Sammy shrugged. 'I'm gay.'

'It's not a crime these days, hasn't been for years. There's no shame in liking men.'

'What do you mean?'

'Well, he could threaten you all he liked, but what was it to him?'

Sammy was shaking his head. 'That's not what I'm saying... John didn't blackmail or threaten me. When he kept raising the fee, Marcin told me to stop paying him. Suggested I go to the cops. And I listened. Went to the cops but they just laughed at me.' He noticed Taylor and snarled. 'I spoke to him. He did nothing. Just laughed at me. Made me feel subhuman.'

'What did you do?'

'I told John where to go. Stopped paying him. Stood firm. Even when the windows got tanned in. Even when my bouncers got the shit kicked out of them. When some arseholes stole my beer delivery. I stood strong through it all.' A fresh tear slid down his cheek. 'Then they killed Marcin. I loved him. Still love him. It's why I drink a bottle of vodka a night. I... I miss him so fucking much.'

'And you're sure it was John McStay?'

'He came into the office, showed me a photo of his body. Dropped Marcin's army dog tags on the desk.' Sammy stared up at the ceiling. 'And that's why I killed John McStay. The world's a better place without him.'

'Okay. Sammy, thank you.' Rakesh locked eyes with him. 'Now, can you let DS Taylor go?'

'Him? No way. I went to him. Told him what happened and he laughed at me. Sat me with this spotty kid. Liam or something. The pair of them just laughed at me. Kept making jokes. Asking me how I took my cock. All of it.'

'Sammy, that's not true!' Taylor's voice was a damp rattle.

'I went to the cops for help and I got laughed at because I'm gay. Said me and my boyfriend were getting picked on for obvious reasons. Even after Marcin died, you covered it up. You denied talking to me about it or knowing anything. Made me think that the cops were in on it, and I knew I'd be next.'

Rakesh held up his hands and dropped his baton

onto the floor. 'Sammy. I want to help you. Just let him go. Murdering won't get you off. Okay?'

Sammy stared at Taylor like he was only just becoming aware that he was holding a knife to the throat of a real, live human being. He let go and tossed the knife behind him.

Taylor collapsed to the floor, grabbing his throat, gasping for air.

Sammy went down on his knees.

Big Craig raced over and grabbed Sammy.

Rakesh shouted, 'Nobody lays a hand on him!'

CHAPTER EIGHTEEN

In truth, a hand or twelve had been laid on Sammy Irvine. A pair of big bruises on his temple were already purple.

Sammy was lowered into the back of a police van. Squad car in front, one behind. Nobody behind the wheels yet, but they were all ready to go.

The sun was close to setting now and the chill had set back in. Some snowflakes floated down, but they weren't lying yet. Supposed to get cold overnight, but Rakesh would be back in Edinburgh. First day in St Leonards tomorrow, meeting his new team. Elliot's old one.

Assuming he wasn't booted off the force.

Rakesh didn't know what to make of it. He'd done some good, but it didn't feel like it.

Elliot smiled at Rakesh. 'Good to see the back of him. Of this whole thing.'

Rakesh could only nod.

Her phone rang. She checked the screen and sighed. 'Better take this.' She walked off, phone to her ear.

A car pulled up and the window wound down. Taylor, his throat covered by white bandages. 'Hey there, Shunty. You okay?'

'I'm fine. You look like you've been through a combine harvester.'

He laughed, way too loud. 'Tell you, I feel like I've stopped to ask directions in Hamilton.'

'I grew up there.'

'Ouch.' Taylor gave Rakesh a hard look. 'Explains a few things.' He looked away. 'Listen, sunshine. You've done well today.'

'Thought you'd be angry with me.'

'Oh, I am.' Taylor laughed. 'But I'm glad you were looking at it from a different angle to the rest of us. If there was a bent cop, I'd want them found. You might not be experienced, but that was good work.'

'It was mostly Kirsten's.'

'Right. Still. Because of you, we found— Well, not Sammy Irvine, but it closed off a few holes in what's happened. We've had a lot of experienced officers running around in circles for a week, heads up their own arseholes, and none of them got to the bottom of what happened. In all truth, I'm glad you raised that with me and Andi. I had you pegged as another useless direct-entry knob but, as well as getting us a lead on him, it's helped me clear my name.' Taylor fixed him with a hard stare. 'Thank you for saving me back there in that flat. I hate to think what he'd have done to me.'

Rakesh couldn't look at him. 'Well.'

'You stopped him. He was going to kill me.'

'I just did what anyone—'

'No. You stood face-to-face with a killer. You talked him down. That takes balls of steel.' Taylor winced. 'Though mine feel like last week's mince right now after he clattered me in them.'

'It's been an education, Callum. Thank you.'

'And you.'

'Did you really say all that to him when he came in?'

'Been through my notebook. We spoke to him. Me and Liam. Flagged it with the organised crime unit. Was going to chase up, then he's wanted for murder.' Taylor honked his horn and held up his arm, running his finger through the air outside of the car. 'Let's get this show on the road, boys!' He winked at Rakesh. 'Hope our paths don't cross again.' He drove off across the car park, his window winding up. 'See you around, Shunty.'

The cars and van followed him.

Rakesh's breath misted in the air.

What a first day.

Losing a murderer. Accusing a decent cop of being corrupt. Catching a murderer. He hoped the rest of the week was going to be easier.

Absolute chaos.

Elliot came back over, prodding her finger off her phone a few times. 'Sodding hell, how do I— There.' She put it away and sighed. 'Okay.'

'Is it good news or bad?'

She shrugged. 'Not mine to say.' She nodded over his shoulder.

A silver Lexus pulled into the car park and a tall man in a sharp suit got out. His quiff looked wet even in the freezing cold, held in place with hair gel. His upper body filled out the suit, but his legs were spindly. He thrust out a hand covered in calluses. 'DCI Jim Pringle. I presume you're DS Siyal?'

'That's me, sir.'

'Well, this *has* been a day, hasn't it?' Pringle laughed. 'When do we transport the prisoner?'

'Already gone, Jim.' Elliot was shivering. 'Just a minute ago.'

'Ah.' Pringle scowled like he was sucking on a lemon. 'Well, do you want the bad news first?'

Elliot folded her arms. 'Go on.'

'We've got that initial confession and a bunch of leads now for Taylor's team to follow up on. The PF's team are... Well, not exactly smiling ear to ear, but pretty pleased.'

Elliot was frowning. 'Are you sure about that?'

'Why?'

Rakesh stepped in, like he was dealing with a senior partner in his old firm. 'Sir, he made some serious allegations against DS Taylor. If there's an audit trail to back them up, it would be a mitigating factor in any conviction. Wouldn't absolve him entirely, but it would go from murder down to manslaughter. A good lawyer could even argue self-defence.'

Pringle scowled. 'Andi?'

'I agree. Any lawyer will get him off. *Any.* There are holes miles wide in the case.'

Rakesh was nodding. 'Sammy Irvine's as much a victim as anyone. He was pushed beyond the limit and took the law into his own hands.'

'Precisely. Few could blame him for what he did, but he still did it. He should spend the rest of his life in prison.' Elliot gave Rakesh some side eye. 'That is, assuming some numpty didn't accidentally let him go.'

Pringle frowned at that. 'Anyway. There is some good news. Someone—' He shot a glance in the direction of the departing cars. '—put in a good word for you, DS Siyal. DS Taylor was impressed with your role in securing both the location of and the confession from Sammy Irvine, if not the conviction of.'

Rakesh felt himself blushing. 'Thank you.'

But there was a massive, heavy-soled, size thirteen boot waiting to drop.

'Well, depends on your perspective, but I am here to tell DI Elliot that I've secured her permanent tenure in the Borders.'

Rakesh looked at Elliot.

She shrugged. 'I live down here, so it's a lot less of a commute. For my sins, I grew up around here. Know the places, know the people. My time in Glasgow and Edinburgh have shown me how important that is.'

Rakesh smiled at her. 'Congratulations, ma'am.'

'Oh, it's not just you.' Pringle was beaming wide. 'Because you did such a good job here, Shunty, I'm basing you down here permanently as well.'

AFTERWORD

Thank you for reading this book – I hope you enjoyed it!

I've been planning this series – my first new police procedural one since 2016 – for a couple of years now and it's a relief to be able to start launching the material I've amassed.

If you've not met DI Rob Marshall yet, you've met all of the supporting characters for the novels and I hope you enjoy the first novel, THE TURNING OF OUR BONES, when you read it.

If you've come to this having read the first book, then I hope this brought some of those other characters to life. Rest assured that book two is done and on preorder now – I hope you enjoy that one too.

Thanks, as always, go to James Mackay for the editing work, which helped tighten and focus the story.

AFTERWORD

Also, huge thanks to John Rickards for copy editing, and to Mare Bate for proofing.

If you notice any errors in the text, which are all my fault, then please email ed@edjames.co.uk and I'll fix them. Thank you!

And if you could leave a review on Amazon? That'd be a huge help, cheers.

Cheers,

Ed James

Scottish Borders, October 2022

ABOUT THE AUTHOR

Ed James writes crime-fiction novels, primarily the DI Simon Fenchurch series, set on the gritty streets of East London featuring a detective with little to lose. His Scott Cullen series features a young Edinburgh detective constable investigating crimes from the bottom rung of the career ladder he's desperate to climb.

Formerly an IT project manager, Ed began writing on planes, trains and automobiles to fill his weekly commute to London. He now writes full-time and lives in the Scottish Borders, with his girlfriend and a menagerie of rescued animals.

If you would like to be kept up to date with new releases from Ed James, please join the Ed James Readers Club.

Connect with Ed online:
Amazon Author page
Website

OTHER BOOKS BY ED JAMES

ROB MARSHALL SERIES

Ed's first new police procedural series in seven years, focusing on DI Rob Marshall, a criminal profiler turned detective. London-based, an old case brings him back home to the Scottish Borders and the dark past he fled as a teenager.

1. THE TURNING OF OUR BONES (Feb. 2023)

Also available is FALSE START, a prequel novella starring DS Rakesh Siyal, is available for **free** to subscribers of Ed's newsletter or on Amazon.

SCOTT CULLEN MYSTERIES SERIES

Eight novels featuring a detective eager to climb the career ladder, covering Edinburgh and its surrounding counties, and further across Scotland.

1. GHOST IN THE MACHINE
2. DEVIL IN THE DETAIL
3. FIRE IN THE BLOOD
4. STAB IN THE DARK

5. COPS & ROBBERS
6. LIARS & THIEVES
7. COWBOYS & INDIANS
8. HEROES & VILLAINS

CULLEN & BAIN SERIES

Six novellas spinning off from the main Cullen series covering the events of the global pandemic in 2020.

1. CITY OF THE DEAD
2. WORLD'S END
3. HELL'S KITCHEN
4. GORE GLEN
5. DEAD IN THE WATER
6. THE LAST DROP

CRAIG HUNTER SERIES

A spin-off series from the Cullen series, with Hunter first featuring in the fifth book, starring an ex-squaddie cop struggling with PTSD, investigating crimes in Scotland and further afield.

1. MISSING
2. HUNTED
3. THE BLACK ISLE

DS VICKY DODDS SERIES

Gritty crime novels set in Dundee and Tayside, featuring a DS juggling being a cop and a single mother.

1. BLOOD & GUTS
2. TOOTH & CLAW
3. FLESH & BLOOD
4. SKIN & BONE
5. GUILT TRIP

DI SIMON FENCHURCH SERIES

Set in East London, will Fenchurch ever find what happened to his daughter, missing for the last ten years?

1. THE HOPE THAT KILLS
2. WORTH KILLING FOR
3. WHAT DOESN'T KILL YOU
4. IN FOR THE KILL
5. KILL WITH KINDNESS
6. KILL THE MESSENGER
7. DEAD MAN'S SHOES
8. A HILL TO DIE ON
9. THE LAST THING TO DIE

Other Books

Other crime novels, with Lost Cause set in Scotland and Senseless set in southern England, and the other three set in Seattle, Washington.

- LOST CAUSE
- SENSELESS
- TELL ME LIES
- GONE IN SECONDS
- BEFORE SHE WAKES

Meet DI Rob Marshall in

THE TURNING OF OUR BONES

The first new Ed James series in seven years starts here.

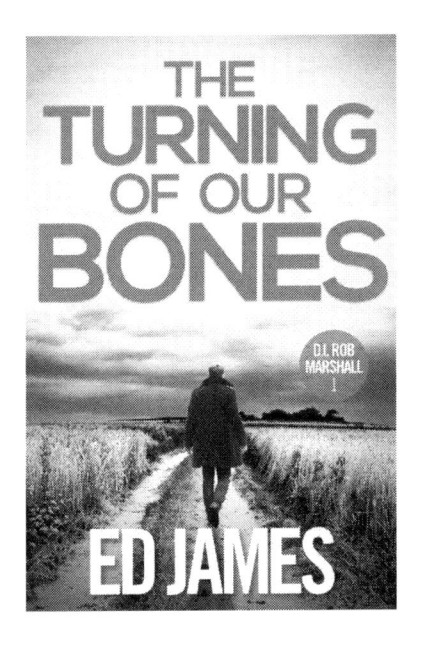

The Serial Killer he couldn't catch is dead...

Can DI Rob Marshall save his last victim before she dies too?

Met cop DI Rob Marshall is hot on the trail of the serial killer known as the Chameleon, who has abducted,

NEXT BOOK

tortured and killed a series of young women in north-west London. As they close in, the Chameleon - who switches identity to get close to his victims - shoots Marshall's partner and escapes.

But when the Chameleon's body is found two years later, Marshall must return to his home town of Melrose in the Scottish Borders and face the tragedy that's haunted him for twenty years, which made him leave in the first place.

The Chameleon's final victim is still missing – can Marshall unpick the Chameleon's latest identity in time to save her from a lonely death?

**Coming
1 February 2023**

Preorder now for a bargain price!

By signing up to my Readers Club, you'll access to **free, exclusive** content (*such as free e-novellas like this*) and keep up-to-speed with all of my releases, by clicking this button:

NEXT BOOK